THE SCROLLS
OF EDESSA

D0631840

THE SCROLLS OF EDESSA

ROBERT L. WISE

VICTOR BOOKS®

A DIVISION OF SCRIPTURE PRESS PUBLICATIONS INC.
USA CANADA ENGLAND

LIBRARY OF CONGRESS CATALOG CARD NUMBER: 87-81018
ISBN: 0-89693-343-1

© 1987 BY SP PUBLICATIONS, INC. ALL RIGHTS RESERVED
PRINTED IN THE UNITED STATES OF AMERICA

COVER ILLUSTRATION: MICHAEL LETWENKO

NO PART OF THIS BOOK MAY BE REPRODUCED
WITHOUT WRITTEN PERMISSION,
EXCEPT FOR BRIEF QUOTATIONS
IN BOOKS AND CRITICAL REVIEWS.

VICTOR BOOKS
A DIVISION OF SP PUBLICATIONS, INC.
WHEATON, ILLINOIS 60187

CONTENTS

Robert L. Wise, Ph.D., is founding pastor of Our Lord's Community Church, Reformed Church of America, in Oklahoma City, Oklahoma. He is the author of several books, including *When There Is No Miracle* and *The Pastors' Barracks*. Dr. Wise has an extensive speaking schedule in the United States and abroad.

To Rachael Marie
who is a gift of pure joy

THE EVIDENCE
OF HISTORY

EUSEBIUS HAS LONG BEEN RECOGNIZED as one of the most important and reliable of the early church fathers and historians. Around 325 he wrote in his *History of the Church* of the correspondence between Jesus and King Abgar V of Edessa. He noted that he had himself personally translated the Syriac documents into Greek.

In the first century, Edessa was a small kingdom within the Parthian Empire. Just beyond the reach of Rome, the surrounding Osrhoene country was a rich and prosperous area. In the modern world the region is now Turkey, and Edessa has become the city of Uria.

Eusebius reports that Abgar V sent a messenger to Jesus imploring Him to come and heal him of an incurable disease. Jesus declined, but promised to send a disciple. Ultimately, the Apostle Thaddaeus came, bringing the shroud with him. This little-known encounter between Abgar and Thaddaeus is one of the remarkable stories of Christian tradition.

Further details of the history and tradition surrounding the shroud's journey to Edessa are recorded in *The Doctrine of Addai*, now in the Imperial Library in Leningrad, Russia.

Robert Wise
Oklahoma City, Oklahoma
1987

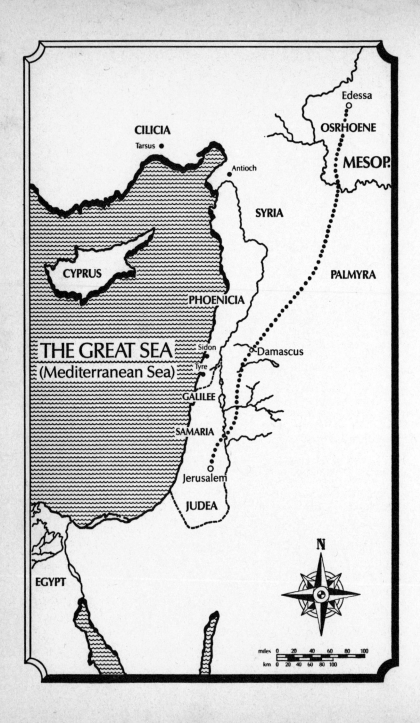

CHAPTER ONE

A.D. 103

I AM A SON telling the father's story. My memories are pieced together with details from others, innuendoes or nuances that veil as much as they reveal. Yet, woven into the plan and fabric of my life is the story of my father's amazing deeds.

The fabric? The cloth?

Yes, of course, you will want to know about the cloth. What can one say of such things except to tell the story. My father's life and the cloth were so interwoven as to be different sides of the same linen. Some felt that to have known the apostle was like touching divinity. Others thought that to see the shroud was to behold Him.

I only remember a father—and the cloth. Near the end of his life, he told me the full story of the dark side of his devotion. But all that is for later. Let us begin at the place where sons learned about sacrifices from their fathers, in that most holy of all cities.

A.D. 34

JERUSALEM

As DUSK RESTED ON THE ROOFTOPS, the moon rose above the horizon line of the surrounding mountains, signaling the end of another day in the holy city of prayer. Quietness settled as the shadows deepened. The evening suddenly felt cool and the air brisk. Annias stood in the doorway watching the soldiers. Had only two years passed since he was last at this very gate? The time had hung so heavily in Egypt that it felt like a decade. He tried to shake off the memory.

Jerusalem was eternally the same and yet, a new atmosphere seemed to enfold him even now. Nothing had changed; everything had changed. Even the cool night air, usually filled with the foul aromas of the marketplace, smelled remarkably fresh. A new wind was blowing.

An abrupt obscenity from a soldier jolted his mind back to the moment at hand. The dangers created by desperate soldier guardians and poverty-stricken thieves of the night caused Annias to stay within the shadows of the stone entryway.

As he watched, the old diplomat thought deeply. Change felt omnipresent. Annias, who prided himself on being an astute analyst, was confounded by the many stories that he heard daily. The strange turn of events was more than he could grasp. He wanted to believe . . . he tried to believe

. . . and yet, he wasn't really sure.

If he had just not lost those months in Egypt, he would have been here when it all happened. But the Romans complicated everything! Because Edessa was beyond their control, they made all the trade negotiations impossible. Just the sight of a soldier was detestable!

Stroking his gray beard, Annias carefully observed the Roman soldiers securing the city gate for the night. The abrasive creaking of the immense hinges resounded through the stone entry as the gate slowly closed on the outside world. Through the narrow passageways of Jerusalem, the sounds of wooden doors being locked and windows being bolted added their hollow notes of suspicion, as the streets quickly emptied.

The slender envoy in the strange turban and rich robes of purple waited until after the soldiers were gone, and then started in an opposite direction. Although Annias was a Jew, his dress and the shape of his beard always caused the residents of Jerusalem to assume he was a Gentile. It served his purposes well to be able to go back and forth between the many worlds of conflict which surrounded him. His distinguished face and regal bearing usually gave him entry anywhere. However, this night his black eyes, deep-set behind gray eyebrows, searched the far corners of the dark alleyways—he wanted to be as inconspicuous as possible.

The winding, labyrinthine streets of Jerusalem always posed a mystery to visitors. The narrow pathways with their stone-encased walls which rose far overhead all looked the same. A wrong turn, and a traveler was hopelessly lost in the maze. Cautiously, Annias traced his steps until he found the right street. He looked in both directions, then moved quickly into a passageway and up the steps. At the top, he crossed over a flat roof and hurried to a large wooden door on the far side. Again, he hesitated before gently rapping. Gifted with a rare blend of caution and daring, Annias always seemed to choose the right moment to hesitate.

A small window in the door opened and someone on the other side awaited a response.

"I am merely seeking the Way," he whispered.

Immediately the small opening shut and the large door opened. Annias was whisked inside and the door quickly bolted.

As he looked from the landing down the stone stairs, he saw candles and torches flickering around a huge gathering room, where long tables were laden with food. People greeted one another with warm embraces, and joy seemed to flow. Everywhere Annias looked, people of all ages were smiling and talking with each other.

"Ah, brother, I do not know you," a swarthy bearded man in very plain robes welcomed him. "Let me greet you."

Immediately the man wrapped his strong arms about Annias' shoulders and robes and gave him an enthusiastic hug. "The kiss of peace is the very expression of God's grace!" he exclaimed joyously.

"Oh, of course," Annias fumbled. "The kiss of peace? Ah, yes, the kiss of peace. I am Annias, a Jew from the far country of Osrhoene in the Parthian Empire."

"Well," the man smiled, "you have indeed come a long way! I am Benjamin. Let us join the believers. How do you know about the Way?"

"I talked with Yeshua when He was in the Galilee."

"Ah, wonderful, wonderful!" Benjamin led him down the steps. "Has not our God done wonderful things?"

Before Annias could answer, a large man who had moved to the center of the head table called out, "Friends, let us gather together for our feast of love!"

People in threadbare robes hugged and shook hands with others in elegant and bright apparel. A man in linen edged with purple handed a piece of fruit to a beggar who leaned on a crutch.

Annias turned to his new acquaintance. "There are no distinctions?"

"Did He not erase all lines?" Benjamin responded solemnly.

"All is His, and He is ours," the leader at the head table pronounced. "Therefore, all is given in the name of His love. Take. Eat."

The words of the prayer rang out, "Boruch Atta Adonai Elohenu Melech ha-olam asher Kidshanu b'mitzvotoz vitslvanu I hadlik ner Shel Yom Tov."

A unanimous "Amen" rang through the room. Since Annias had no expectation of a group response, his Amen sounded after the chorus.

"Shema, Yisrael!" the leader proclaimed with his arms extended.

Immediately the group responded, "Shema Yisrael Adonai Elohenu Adonai Eihad—The Lord our God is one God!"

"In the name of the risen Messiah, then let us begin," the leader invited.

People began eating as they continued talking together. Annias found himself moving through the group as if he had always been one of them.

When Annias again saw Benjamin, he asked with an air of one who understands more than he really knows, "How is the work going?"

"Oh, very well," Benjamin replied. "You know, it is demanding, taking care of all of the problems of the widows and the poor. However, our newly appointed young men are doing very well. You know about Stephen's death?"

"Somewhat," Annias answered, without any idea of who Stephen was. "I have been out of the city and have only recently returned."

"Of course, Stephen's death frightened the people,"

Benjamin explained, "and many left for Galilee and Judea. However, I think the authorities have retreated some since then. The stoning hurt the Sanhedrin's standing with the general population."

Annias nodded his head as if he understood it all. He had the shrewd ways of an elder diplomat who could elicit volumes of information with a few nods and smiles.

"The Romans," Benjamin continued, as he reached for a piece of fish, "think that the Sanhedrin was mad to have caused all of this furor!"

"Never have I seen a city in such a ferment," Annias agreed. "The resurrection story, the miracles, the preaching have surely turned everything upside down."

"People swarm around us to hear about Yeshua," added Benjamin. "I teach of the Messiah to all who sit near the Damascus Gate."

"Marvelous," Annias replied. "And what do you teach them?" While he carefully followed the conversation, he continually watched the movement throughout the room.

As the food was consumed, the tables were cleared. Gradually the group began singing simple songs. The harmony and deep devotion carried through the air as the songs took on a stirring, emotional quality. They sang in a number of different languages at the same time and with seemingly different tunes, producing an uncanny harmony that amazed Annias. Something undefinable was happening in the room and to him. A new and extraordinary Presence, a special Personality, was arising that was much more than a group spirit. Annias found that the singing impelled him to become one with that transcendent Spirit. No longer an official observer, he discovered himself being swept into the center of worship and praise.

Time had lost all meaning when he became aware that the leader at the center table was interrupting the singing. Lifting up the round of bread, he proclaimed, "In this very room, on the night that Yeshua was betrayed, He took the affikomen and broke it. He gave it to us saying, 'This is My body broken for you.' Tonight He offers Himself to us again."

He tore the disk in half and handed it to the men on each side of him. As they each took a piece, they began moving through the room handing out small fragments to all the people. Amens and affirmations rang through the room. Annias felt himself once more carried away by an intensity of devotion.

The leader then picked up a large wooden goblet. Holding it high, he proclaimed, "Yeshua also said, 'This is My blood of the new covenant which I shed for you.' He promised to be here among us when we do this. Is He not with us tonight?"

Amens ringing, the group moved back into song. As the men at the head table moved through the room, each person took a sip from the cup and then returned to singing praise.

When the songs slowly faded, the group once more began to exchange the embrace that Benjamin had called the kiss of peace. After the leader gave a benediction, people began leaving until the group shrunk to about twenty people. Then Annias saw someone he knew.

"You are Thaddaeus!" he said expectantly. "One of the Twelve?"

"Yes," the tall muscular man replied warmly. "I remember seeing you before. Was it not when we were in Galilee? Yes, now I recall. You talked privately with the Master."

"Marvelous!" Annias pumped his hand. "I have found someone who remembers!"

"You must forgive us," Thaddaeus smiled. His sincerity and personable manner were reassuring. "So many came to talk with Yeshua that it is not always easy to remember what was said." Although he was a young man, his liquid brown eyes and confident manner made him seem much older.

"But surely He told you about our conversation?" Annias probed anxiously.

"I'm sorry, but I don't recall," the apostle answered kindly.

"He didn't tell you that He would send someone to heal our king?" Annias persisted.

"Now, now," Thaddaeus answered hesitantly. He was obviously well acquainted with many such inquiries. "Don't worry. We can deal with all this in due time. Let us not be anxious about tomorrow, just as the Master instructed."

"Please, you must help me!" His voice had taken on an uncharacteristic tone of urgency.

"Of course," Thaddaeus answered, with the warm glow of the evening still hovering about him. "This matter must be of unusual importance to you. I will make your need my special concern."

"Let me say more," Annias grasped Thaddaeus by the wrist that he might not leave. "I have come here to seek fulfillment of the promise that Yeshua gave me."

"Yeshua *promised* you?"

"I am here because the Master told me that someone would be sent to help my king. Your leaders must hear my plea."

"You do, indeed, present a serious matter," and the young man's face became thoughtful. "However, it is much too late to talk of such matters tonight. It would be better to hear you tomorrow. Come back in the morning and I will help you then."

"When? At what hour?" the diplomat pressed.

"We will be back here at the fourth hour after prayers at the temple," Thaddaeus explained. "I will talk with you more then."

18

Before Annias could thank him, the apostle pulled away and was gone. Annias found himself moving with the rest of the crowd toward a back door and out into another dark alleyway.

To avoid giving the appearance of having been together as a group, they dispersed in many directions. Back on the empty streets, Annias found himself perplexed and confused by the events of the evening. Although he was not exactly sure what he had experienced, he knew definitely that he had found the people he was seeking.

He believed. . . . And he wanted to believe. . . . He tried to believe. . . . And yet, he wasn't sure. As he walked down the stone alleyway, Annias found his mind racing back in time to a day three years before when he came with a letter from King Abgar to a man who was rumored to be the great healer. Some said that the Nazarene was the Messiah every Jew looked for. Annias recalled the incredible probing in His eyes that appeared to read thoughts before they were uttered. His words had seemed more like poetry than conversation. Surely His presence had been its own statement! Then he remembered the girl who had died and who now lived. This he had seen with his own eyes.

Annias paused at the end of the alley before he moved quickly on. Two years before when he left the teacher, he had been fully ready to believe he was the Messiah. Now, there were all of these new stories which he was not prepared to evaluate. The trial, the shameful death, the reappearance alive again! Mystery followed mystery. As he walked, he could feel the swirling turmoil of Jerusalem pulsating through his own being. He tried to believe. And yet, he wasn't sure.

The next morning well before the appointed hour, Annias returned to the meeting place. With the early light streaming through the upper windows, he sat in a corner reflecting on all that had happened the night before. Although undefinable, something special hovered about this room. A young boy entered the room carrying a bowl of fruit.

"May I get you some refreshment?" he asked, extending the bowl.

"Oh, thank you," Annias answered, noting the plainness of the boy and the wooden bowl. He was accustomed to more regal service.

"I am John Mark and I live here," the boy volunteered cheerfully. "If I can help you, please call."

Again Annias thanked him and watched him disappear behind a coarse, hanging curtain. How different Jerusalem was from Edessa! Situated in the mountains, Jerusalem was filled with pines and tall trees; Edessa sat in the hot, flat plains which were much more barren.

Being here made Annias realize what the Roman occupation meant. Jerusalem reflected the strain and hardship that comes from the heavy hand of an oppressor. Edessa was a proud and free city-state, beyond the control of the Roman legions. Annias knew he would always prefer the allegiance Edessa had with the Parthians to any arrangement which could ever be made with Rome. At that moment an unexpected tinge of homesickness ran through his mind. He allowed it to linger only for an instant, then banished it.

As his eyes focused again on the room, Annias wondered what might have been his fate if his forefathers had not been driven from Jerusalem generations before. The kings of Edessa had been quick to recognize the intelligence and cleverness of his ancestors. Never knowing anything but life in the shadow of the palace, Annias and his family had always been the special confidants of kings. Being Jewish had kept them separate from the power struggles of the royal bloodlines and above petty, local conflict. Yes, life in Edessa had been very good to them.

Even more than his privileged position, Annias genuinely loved the king. Yes, Abgar was arrogant, but he was a benevolent ruler who sought the best for the people. Annias felt pain in knowing how important it was that the king survive and stability continue.

"Good morning, brother!" rang from the top of the stairs.

Startled, Annias looked up to see Thaddaeus. Wearing a dark brown robe the color of his hair and beard, Thaddaeus had a plain, unadorned appearance. As was Annias' habit, he studied the face before responding, and saw that this man was anything but simple. A genuine handsomeness and forceful masculinity was written into his piercing brown eyes and powerfully set jaw. In addition, Annias could sense his quick mind.

"Peace be with you!" Thaddaeus smiled as he descended the stairs and wrapped his arms about Annias in what must have been another of those confounded kisses of peace.

Uncomfortable but compliant, Annias mumbled, "*Shalom Aleichem*," as he attempted to return an embrace of sorts. Annias generally kept people at arm's length, and disliked the emotional closeness of hugging.

"The group will be here shortly." Thaddaeus' tone changed abruptly. "What can I help you with?"

Sensing that he could come to his point immediately, Annias stretched to his full height and slightly moved on his toes. "I am a special courier and ambassador from King Abgar V, the Sovereign of Edessa and the Protector of Osrhoene. My gracious sovereign owes no allegiances save to the Parthians!"

Thaddaeus' eyes narrowed and he pursed his lips as he settled back on a bench.

"I come in the name of His Illustrious Majesty and speak as his voice," and Annias swept his robe back in a manner calculated to intimidate and create compliance.

Thaddaeus interrupted, holding up his hand in a gesture

that demanded silence, "You said you were a Jew?"

Annoyance crossed Annias' face and irritation slipped into his words. "I *am* Jewish, but the king has given me—"

Once again Thaddaeus' hand pushed the pretension aside, making the old man appear awkward. "How does a Jew come to us from this faraway place?"

"My family went to the land of Osrhoene during the Dispersion. By God's goodness we have prospered and been allowed to serve the king. Yet we have always remained faithful Jews and keepers of the Law."

Thaddaeus motioned for the envoy to sit down. Just then, the hanging curtain swayed suspiciously. "John Mark!" A sheepish looking boy emerged from behind the curtain. "Your habit of eavesdropping has already gotten you into enough trouble, hasn't it?" He abruptly pulled the boy forward. "I suggest that you go downstairs immediately and help your mother."

The boy disappeared behind the curtain and scampered down the stone stairs. At the same moment the upper door opened and people began filing in.

"Now," Thaddaeus turned back, "you say that you personally talked with Yeshua and He told you something?"

"Oh, more than that." Annias leaned forward, pressing the apostle. "He gave me a promise."

Thaddaeus' face was serious. "Of course, any word the Master uttered is of the most urgent importance to be taken with deepest concern." Leaning back, he carefully measured his words. "I'm sure you can appreciate that we must cautiously consider what has been reported as coming from His mouth, to make sure there is no misunderstanding."

Silence fell between them, as the solemn face of the apostle was Annias' answer. Pomp had not impressed nor unique claim confounded him.

"I would not lie." Annias' sudden transparency surprised even him.

For the first time Thaddaeus smiled and nodded approvingly. "We shall see," and he patted the older man's hand. "We shall see to your request. But now an unexpected concern is before us. You may stay and listen, and I will introduce you to the believers."

The room was filled with people seated around the room waiting for someone to speak. Thaddaeus moved from the bench to the center. "Shalom."

"Shalom Aloeheim," rang back.

"Our hearts are heavy at the departure of our brother Alexander from this life." Thaddaeus spoke as one who is the leader. "We bless his memory and the special part he played in the story of our Lord. His wife, Joanna, will be with us shortly. However, I first want to present a new friend who has come to us from the far country of Osrhoene. Come, Annias, and meet our group."

Quickly and elegantly Annias swept to the front. "My sovereign, King Abgar V, who sent me to find Yeshua, sends his greeting to the followers of the Way. . . ." He paused, realizing that a show of diplomatic pontification would not impress these people. ". . . and I talked with Him two years ago. It was then that I met Thaddaeus."

A murmur of appreciation went around the room. Thaddaeus nodded his head, as Annias continued.

"My king has been deteriorating, from an incurable disease, for some years. If no cure is found, he will soon die. Even in our far country we had heard of the mighty works of Yeshua of Nazareth, and I was sent to come to inquire of Yeshua for healing our king."

Once more the group nodded as if they were hearing a familiar story which had been repeated by other dignitaries.

"I met with Yeshua privately," Annias thumped his chest, "and was deeply touched by Him. We talked for many hours of the kingdom." Sensing the group's sympathies with him, he moved toward the heart of the matter.

"He told me that He could not come, but that He would send a disciple to minister to the king and to our people."

The room became intensely silent. Waiting a moment for the full effect, Annias' eyes flashed. "He promised!"

Another long pause filled the room. "And your country and king are Jewish?" a voice in the back of the room asked.

His face went blank. All the envoy could do was shake his head negatively.

"Thank you." Thaddaeus gently pushed him from behind. "We will look forward to knowing you as one of us. For now, we speak of and pray about the death of Alexander."

Annias' shoulders dropped as he found himself being directed to the back of the group. He lost the rest of what was being said by the apostle. The moment seemed to have run through his fingers and vanished. His mouth felt dry.

Taking a seat by the back wall, he wasn't sure of what to do next. Instinctively he knew that he needed to obtain some special influence.

The curtains parted once more and young John Mark moved through the group offering service and refreshment. The little eavesdropper seemed to know just when to appear.

The little eavesdropper? What better ally might he have than someone who seemed to know all the details of what was being said privately? As the lad came toward the edge of the group, Annias found a coin in his purse.

"John Mark, isn't it?" he asked in a whisper.

"Oh, yes," the bright eyes sparkled.

'Well, we must become friends. Perhaps, a cup of cold water would be good," he said as he pressed the coin into the boy's palm. Delight was more than evident as the little servant dashed off for the kitchen.

Just then, the curtain parted again and a woman wearing a cloak and hood came through. The hood covered her face,

hiding her eyes. In her arms was a la
rope. She walked to the center of the
on the table, and sat down.

Thaddaeus reached down tenderl
der. "Joanna, our love and prayers
grieve for Alexander. His untimely d

Joanna squeezed his hand, only nodding
eyes remained veiled, as Thaddaeus continued, "Alexander
was the faithful steward of Joseph of Arimathea. Even
though he was a Greek, he was never a Gentile to us. On
that final Friday, he helped prepare Yeshua's body for
burial. Joanna, how can we help you?"

She rose to her feet slowly. Still leaning on the table with
her eyes cast down, she pushed the bundle toward
Thaddaeus. "Thank you," she said quietly. "We had hoped
for the return of the Lord before we would see death ever
again. But Alexander instructed me that should he die, I
was to give you the cloth. He said the apostles would know
what should be done."

"The cloth?" Thaddaeus reached for the bundle. "I don't
understand."

"In the afternoon of the day our Lord arose, Joseph and
Alexander returned to the tomb to look once again. Only
then did they realize the burial clothes were still there.
Joseph was perplexed about what to do." Joanna turned to
the whole group. "Were they the clothes of the grave or had
they become garments of life?" Her voice fell. "Being a Jew,
Joseph did not want to touch the shroud, so he instructed
Alexander to dispose of it."

As the eyes of the whole group turned toward the strange
bundle, Thaddaeus withdrew his hand.

"What do you mean?" Thaddaeus asked. "What are you
saying, Joanna?"

"Alexander didn't destroy the cloth. Before he died, he
instructed me to bring you the burial cloth of Yeshua."

JOANNA STOOD UP and reached for the bundle. "I didn't want to handle it either. But Alexander said this cloth was different."

Although she pushed the package toward Thaddaeus, he did not move. Silence continued to hang in the air. As her hood fell back, Joanna pulled on the rope that bound the bundle together.

"Alexander did not explain. He simply said, 'There is life here.' " She untied the knot and separated the bindings. "Now we must learn what he and Joseph discovered that afternoon."

No one moved. Only Annias bent to one side to get a clearer view of the cloth. Joanna slowly peeled back the crude piece of dull canvas that contained a folded linen.

"I will need help to unwrap the cloth . . . Alexander reasoned that no one could be contaminated by anything that had touched our Lord." Her eyes searched their faces.

"He felt it was like being touched by the crucifixion again. Therefore, I knew I must carefully honor his request that the shroud be entrusted to the apostles."

26

She lifted the linen out of its container and looked at Thaddaeus. "I bring it that you may seek the counsel of the Twelve."

When Thaddaeus did not respond, Joanna slowly began to unfold the bundle. "Surely you cannot fear touching what has held the Lord?" she chided the group. "We have handled the cloth on a number of occasions, and God's wrath has not fallen on us. Here, help me." She handed a corner to one person and then another edge to someone else. A very long, single piece of cloth began to unwind. The cloth was fourteen feet long and over three feet wide. Although the herringbone pattern of the linen was the common weave, the cloth was so fine it seemed almost like silk. Across the surface could be seen the sepia stains of the spices and ointments and the dark discolorations of dried blood.

"On the night of the crucifixion," Joanna said, as she pulled the cloth taut, "half of the shroud was unrolled for the body to be laid flat on it. Then the rest was doubled back over the top of the body, holding the lifeless form of the Master as if it were in a pocket."

As they watched the full length of the shroud unfold, one of the men rose to his feet in protest. "Something is wrong here. This was not the proper way to have buried the Lord."

"Yes," a prosperous looking man added. "Only common people are covered with such a single piece of cloth. There should have been other special preparations."

"Can you explain, Joanna?" a dignified man in the rear of the group asked.

"It was very late, and the Sabbath was upon us. We had no time to do more." For a moment she stared off at some distant point in the room. "I recall that Joseph told us to remember that He had made Himself to be one with us in every common way. He felt that Yeshua would have preferred to be prepared in the same way as would have been done for one of the least. Joseph felt the simplicity was appropriate."

"Is this really necessary?" Thaddaeus asked, finally moving forward. "I see no need for us to examine this cloth. The Law of Moses still forbids what we are doing. This is not seemly!"

"No, wait!" One of the men came to his feet pointing at the center. "Pull it tighter! Hold it upright!" As the men held the cloth up like a flag, the bright light of morning fell over its entirety.

The group stared in amazement. A clear outline revealed the full-length impression of the front and the back of a man's body. On one end they could see the powerful chest with the arms and hands crossed over the abdomen. The faint but clear countenance of a majestic face seemed to be burned into the cloth. Here and there the blood and fluid stains completed the picture of a body that had been beaten and tortured. Extending to the other end of the shroud was the imprint of the underside of the body. The lashes of the whip had now been transferred into the cloth as the wounds left long, dark bloodstains.

Yet each person saw something more; almost as if a hot iron had seared a brown burn, an image had been left on the shroud. A faint, yellowish brown glow seemed etched into the cloth itself. It was as though an unearthly radiation had forever imprinted the face and form of the Messiah on the cloth.

Time stopped as the morning light moved across the shroud. The silence seemed strangely broken by what they were seeing.

"This is what Alexander wanted you to know," Joanna's voice was quiet but intense. "At the moment of resurrection this record was left. The shroud is a picture of Rabboni as His life returned."

"No, no!" Thaddaeus interrupted. "As the law demands, it must be quickly burned or buried. To do more is to invite scandal."

"The body *is* naked," a pained voice added. "Nothing is hidden."

"The nude body of the Lord must not be seen," Thaddaeus' gesture pushed the cloth away. "We have enough difficulty explaining the death on a cross. A naked figure can only make matters worse!"

"This is the Lord," Joanna spoke to the whole group as well as to Thaddaeus. "Can we destroy such a picture?"

Unnoticed, Annias had made his way through the group to the front of the room. Without touching the cloth, he gently reached his hand near to the face and bent over the cloth.

"He really did live again!" he uttered with an awe that no one noticed.

"This could become a graven image." Thaddaeus was beginning to look hostile. "The Sanhedrin would have grounds to crucify all of us! Should word of this object spread through Jerusalem, there would be no end to the uproar."

"But only God could have fashioned such a thing," another man added. "How can we ignore what He has ordained?"

Throwing up his hands in dismay, Thaddaeus turned his back. Annias sank down on the bench and lowered his head into his hands. The rest of the group silently stared at the cloth.

Finally Annias addressed the men. "People who know nothing of the God of Abraham, Isaac, and Jacob, of the covenant or of Yeshua, would be greatly helped to see such an object."

"Helped?" Thaddaeus turned, mystified.

"Oh, yes!" Annias insisted. "In a country such as mine,

the cloth would be quickly understood and believed as a help to faith."

"Faith must come from hearing, not seeing," Thaddaeus retorted, feeling irritation that this outsider was even speaking in the debate.

"Yeshua did say that it is more blessed to have believed without seeing," a dignified man added, trying to sound less abrasive than Thaddaeus.

"But I tell you," Annias insisted, "the day is coming when you are going to have to explain your faith in a much bigger world than the one you now live in. You cannot know what such an object could mean to them."

Joanna stepped to the cloth and let her hand carefully touch the edge feeling the texture. "I wonder if He has also given us this evidence to help at some other time when people will need to see, for reasons we cannot understand today."

"But it shows His nude body," one of the men insisted.

"Friends, we must remember that other places in the world look at these things differently!" Feeling that he had now reached the limits of propriety, Annias stopped and once more lowered his head into his hands.

Finally, Thaddaeus again faced the group. "Brothers, we must carefully consider all of these matters. No one can know how much is at stake here. I think we must pray separately and together before we will even know how to proceed."

The group murmured agreement.

Thaddaeus placed his big, strong hand on Annias' shoulder. The richness of the stranger's robes made striking contrast with his own dress. "My friend, twice in one day you have confounded us." His eyes narrowed. "Perhaps this is good and maybe it is not. Certainly we will have to discuss the matter privately." After a long pause, a smile inched up one side of his face. "Who is equal to these things? So much has changed so quickly. Well, maybe Abba is bent on changing all the rules!"

The men gathered the corners of the cloth together and folded it back into a bundle. Following the prayer, the group dispersed through the curtain that concealed the back stairway. Annias stood in the shadow watching Thaddaeus secure the strange package.

As he tucked the bundle inside the covering, the apostle reflected on the bizarre turn of events. The more he thought of it, the more unsure he was about what he ought to do. Should the shroud be treated with reverence, or was it just an awful residue of a painful night of agony? Should they really be worshipful before this reminder of sacrifice, or was it a violation of the law? As he pulled the rope tight to tie a knot, a finger was thrust into the center of the ropes. "That will make it easier," Annias said.

"Thank you," and Thaddeus kept his eyes lowered.

"We must hurry," Annias continued. "We have much to speak of and do before your next meeting with the Twelve."

"We?" Thaddaeus' head jerked up.

"Yes, of course," and the clever diplomat smiled.

Once again the light of a new day streamed through the high side windows as the people left the room. Annias was surprised how many of them he had come to know during the last week. He also realized there was an almost dreamlike quality to his reflections. He felt as if an avalanche had swept away the person he had been, and someone new and not yet defined was appearing. So many ideas, so many unexpected thoughts, so much redefinition . . . and now today's teachings piled on top of this amorphous heap of newness!

"No man can serve two masters." The diplomat could not keep the apostle's words from ringing in his ears. "My,

31

my," he erupted aloud, "there is great demand here!"

"What?" an old woman turned. "What did you say?" Her wrinkled eyes blinked.

"Oh, nothing," Annias assured her. "Just thinking out loud. . . ." Suddenly John Mark burst out from behind the curtain and darted between them as if off on some secret or clandestine mission.

"The teaching was wonderful today," the old woman tugged at his sleeve, "but I don't hear very well so I must sit near the front." She kept smiling, nodding, blinking.

"Yes, yes." Annias nervously surveyed the room realizing that in the exchange he had lost sight of Thaddaeus. "Excuse me," he bowed graciously, "I must find someone."

As he moved through the crowd, Annias felt certain that Thaddaeus was gone. "I know he is trying to lose me," he said to himself. "I've been pressing him too closely these last five days."

When John Mark again went speeding past, Annias grabbed the back of his robe. "Where has Thaddaeus gone?"

"Oh, he left even before the teaching was finished."

"Ah!" Annias exclaimed aloud. "I knew he was trying to avoid me!"

"Can I be of service?" John Mark suggested, eyeing the little coin pouch dangling at Annias' waist.

"You are a boy of great promise. Find my friend for me and it will be worth your time."

Like a stone shot from a slingshot, the bright-eyed spy was through the curtain and down the stairs to the alleyway which led to the street, leaving Annias to his thoughts.

"Could you help me?" an unfamiliar voice inquired.

Annias turned to find a strikingly beautiful young woman next to him. The carefully combed flow of her hair and the fragrance of an expensive perfume set her apart from so many who came to the gatherings. Her beauty had a regal quality that obviously allured and could make a man her captive.

"Whatever you wish!" Annias offered with a sweeping movement of his arm and a slight bow.

"I am looking for one of the leaders, a man called Thaddaeus," she said, and her black eyes sparkled.

"My, my," Annias smiled. "Thaddaeus is a popular man today!"

"Do you know him?" her inviting smile seemed out of place.

"He and I are good friends," Annias suggested with his own interest in mind, "but I am afraid he has already left. However, I am sure he would want *me* to help you on his behalf."

"There is so much I do not understand about your new movement. I need someone to instruct me and help me in the Way."

"May I ask your name?"

"My name?" she answered with a flirtatious air. "You've not seen me in your meetings before?" Her manner contrasted sharply with other women in the group.

Annias took full measure of the small woman whose raven black hair framed a face that could have been on the statue of a Greek goddess. Standing there in her rich flowing robes, she conveyed the sophistication of one who has reached a significant station in life. She seemed, like himself, to be able to step out of the Jewish world and rise above narrow provincialism. She was adroit enough to be alluring without suggesting more than she intended. Annias admired such capacities almost as much as he appreciated the womanliness wrapped in the purple-edged gown.

"No," he smiled. "You've not been here before. However, I can certainly handle your questions." He glanced around making sure no one was observing his deceptive performance.

"Do you really believe that this Yeshua is truly *ha Mashiach*, the Messiah?" Her question was sudden, direct and unveiled.

"Why—ah, why, yes—yes."

"Why?" Although her voice was quiet, her eyes seemed strangely hostile. She leaned toward him.

Annias stepped back rather unsteadily. "I did meet Him while traveling in the north several years ago." He stroked at his beard, "I—ah—also listened to His teachings. Truly, I had never seen such a man as this."

"Now you are obviously more intelligent than most of this uneducated rabble," her voice was low and almost purred. "Do you *really* think that He did the miracles they claim?"

Annias shifted his weight clumsily from one foot to the other. "I can tell you honestly that I have talked with people who were sick and now are well." Annias could feel his tone changing from fascination to seriousness. "I met a child that they said was once dead who now lives."

"Well," she laughed, "we are Sadducees. Death is death," she tossed aside casually. "We certainly don't believe in resurrection."

"I saw a cloth—" he blurted and then stopped. "Perhaps, it would be best to have you talk to some of the group who were eyewitnesses to these matters."

"No!" she said curtly. "I want to talk with Thaddaeus— and no one else."

"Oh?" his head turned sideways. "*Only* Thaddaeus?" She made no response of any kind.

"Well," he hesitated for a moment, "when I see him next, I will tell Thaddaeus that someone wants to talk about miracles."

"No!" a sly smile crossed her face, "just tell him Alicia wants to see him." With that, she whirled around and walked up the stairs that led to the upper door. Not once did she look back. Annias had the distinct feeling that he had been turned into the servant boy.

The shadows were falling across the alleyways and the narrow streets were darkening when Annias finally found the apostle. With feet placed wide apart and hands defiantly set on his hips, he glared at Thaddaeus. Totally ignoring the imposing figure standing before him, the apostle continued talking with the ragged street vendor, put his arm about him, and quietly prayed a benediction on their conversation. Then he turned to Annias.

"Sit down, my friend," he patted the large rock on which he had reclined, "and rest. You have not yet learned how to be free of anxiety and to leave all things in His hands."

Annias bristled and didn't move. "I needed to talk with you earlier today!" He flung his arms in the air. "You disappeared!"

"There is a time to be together, and there is a time to be apart."

"Humph!" Annias said indignantly. "You also missed an important person who wants to talk with you."

"Who?"

"A magnificent woman with rare beauty. Obviously her background is of the highest class."

"So?" Thaddaeus only smiled.

"Her name is Alicia."

The apostle's body stiffened and his face froze.

"Well, now I *do* appear to have your attention for a change!"

"What did she want?"

"There must be quite a story here," Annias taunted him.

"What did she want?" Thaddaeus pulled the older man close to him. His eyes flashed.

"To speak to you, to speak to you," he apologized. "And

to know more about the Way," he added as an after-thought.

Thaddaeus' icy stare made Annias realize he had again misjudged a situation. The apostle's silence became intense.

"That is absolutely all she said," Annias fumbled.

"Leave her alone," Thaddaeus warned. "She could be the source of great trouble."

Standing up, Thaddaeus began backing away from Annias. His glare clearly meant that he was not to be followed. He pointed his finger at Annias and said, "Do not tell her you have seen me!"

In the days that followed, Annias found it impossible to see Thaddaeus alone. During the closed meetings of the apostles, Annias camped outside the door, waiting for him to appear. He kept sending in messages about his request for someone to come to Edessa, but he had no idea if they even discussed his need—or the shroud and its meaning.

Feeling defeated and old, Annias started walking across the roof toward the stairs that would lead him back onto the street. He thought how strange it was that whenever the new woman appeared, Thaddaeus disappeared.

Slowly, carefully, going down the steps, he pondered how his own opinion of the woman had changed. At first she had sat in the back of the room and was clearly cynical. But in the last day or so, she had moved to the front and was listening intensely. Her aloofness and condescension were gone, and at times she even seemed like a little girl from one of the villages. Stopping near the bottom step, he thought, "Thaddaeus is wrong; she doesn't intend harm."

As he wandered out on the stone street, Annias turned the corner onto one of the broader thoroughfares where the merchants and vendors spread their wares. "Something very personal is going on" he thought.

Leaning up against the rough stone wall that framed the street, he watched the women and their little ones. Children were chasing each other in and out of the stalls as their mothers tested the fruit and examined the vegetables. He had never married and often felt the loneliness of a solitary meal and an empty bed. Although Annias had known many women intimately, he was devoted only to the king, and knew that marriage and children would never grace his life.

"I wonder if Thaddaeus thinks of such things," he mused. Immediately, the alluring face of Alicia came back to mind and two images floated before his eyes. He could see her calculating look as she said, "Just tell him Alicia wants to see him." That recollection merged and blurred with the memory of how the apostle appeared as he warned, "Do not tell her you have seen me."

"M-m-m," hummed deep in his throat as he walked aimlessly through the crowds. "Thaddaeus never speaks of women," he observed out loud.

The next morning Annias hurried to the upper room for the teaching. The dry heat of summer could already be felt even at this early hour. As Annias made his way up the back steps, he realized that people were being screened as they reached the landing. Here and there the familiar faces of leaders could be seen watching the whole area. While they struck a casual pose, Annias could detect their intense scrutiny of every person who went past.

Crossing the threshold, he started down the steps into the large room when he saw Alicia. Lovely as always, she did not fade into the crowd. She could not be missed. Yet she did not seem as flashy and alluring as she had the first time she had come to the meetings. Immediately Annias looked for Thaddaeus, but he was nowhere to be seen.

Pausing on the steps a moment longer, he looked a second time.

The press of people behind him pushed Annias on down into the room and toward the back. His eyes kept darting back and forth seeking his friend. When the last person was in and the door was bolted, and ominous sound sent a hush through the room. One of the men then stood by the door near a peephole.

From behind the curtain a large rugged man suddenly appeared. The crowd murmured approval and then broke into applause. Everyone seemed to know him except Annias. A ripple of applause arose from the group. "Welcome, Simon," some called out.

"Grace and peace be unto you!" The man held up his hand in a gesture of blessing. "The promises of the Lord are being fulfilled!"

"Hallelujah! Hoshiahnna!" rang back from the crowd.

The leader put a finger to his lips to indicate the need for quietness. "Let us pray silently," he instructed, and closed his eyes. For several minutes the room was encased in total silence. Finally the man said simply, "Amen."

As the group settled onto the floor or the few benches around the room, the man began to speak. "First, I must warn you that another wave of persecution is upon us. Those who killed Stephen are even now on their way to Damascus to attack the saints; we must pray for our brothers and also be cautious of being followed. Let us return to prayer and intercede for the people of God."

He began a prayer for the protection of believers in Jerusalem, Samaria, and Damascus. Others joined in spontaneously and even Annias found himself muttering his own prayers of intercession as he lost all sense of the flow of time.

When he opened his eyes as the prayer ended, Annias discovered that John Mark had crept up to his side. And

John Mark never made such appearances without good reason.

"Thaddaeus is listening behind the curtain," he said in a whisper. "I thought you might want to know," and he held his hand out expectantly. Annias swiftly moved through the crowd and across the back of the room. Once he reached the edge of the drape, he paused a moment and then darted behind the curtain.

"Why are you hiding from us?" he blurted as he abruptly stood face to face with the apostle. "I am your friend."

As if fearing the sound would carry into the room, Thaddaeus drew back from the entrance down the dim hallway, but Annias only pressed him more closely.

"Perhaps I am too forceful," the old man whispered, "but I want to be of service to you."

Thaddaeus only retreated farther into the passageway.

"I know there is something between you and the woman. At first I was insensitive and I apologize," Annias pleaded, "but I want to assist you as best I can."

The hallway narrowed and became darker as the apostle continued to retreat. Although Annias could barely see Thaddaeus' eyes, the pain in his words was clear. "You have no idea who she is and why she is seeking me out! She must be avoided."

"Why?"

"Because I think she may be here only to spy on us."

"I have watched her for many days now," Annias said defiantly, "and she is not a spy."

"How do you know?" his voice had an edge. "I am very well acquainted with her husband's opinions and I know that he hates us." The apostle sounded hot and bitter.

Annias grabbed Thaddaeus' cloak. "I *tell* you she is no spy!"

"They are Sadducees and believe we are troublemakers

and seditionists." Thaddaeus breathed into the envoy's face.

"The first time I met her, she told me she was a Sadducee and that she did not believe. She has made no pretense with us."

"What do you know of her pretense?" Thaddaeus scowled.

"If she is not a spy, then what right do you have to turn her away? How can you be so sure that God is not a part of her coming here?"

Silence was the apostle's only answer.

"Well?" Annias persisted. "Do you have all the answers to everything? Whether or not she is a spy, you cannot keep running away from talking with her. She is not going to disappear."

"I have prayed about the matter," Thaddaeus stepped back, "but—I—ah—I do not yet have an answer. I am sorry." His voice fell. "I just don't know what to do." The words were much softer.

"But you can't keep hiding from her!" Annias bore in. "You must face her today."

"Look," Thaddaeus pleaded, "don't you understand the warning that has just been given?"

"I understand what I have seen in your eyes and face," Annias said kindly. "You fear this woman for more reasons than you are saying."

Thaddaeus turned away and started to leave. "Do not fear me," Annias pleaded. "I have kept the confidence of kings and I have as much at stake here as you do. You can trust me."

Annias hung onto the back of Thaddaeus' robe and kept him from going farther. "You are the only person who can determine whether or not she is a spy. If you really believe she is, then you must protect all of us!" When the robe went limp, the diplomat knew he had found the argument that would finally settle the whole matter.

"I can't!" Thaddaeus protested.

"You can and you must!" Annias insisted. "All of us must have the protection of knowing the truth about this woman. You have an obligation to find out if she is a spy."

Slowly the apostle turned around. The long pause that followed seemed like an eternity to Annias. Finally Thaddaeus walked back to the curtain and then slumped back against the wall, as if listening to the teaching coming from the other side of the barrier. Obviously his mind was elsewhere.

When the meeting ended, the two men stepped from behind the curtain and made their way through the group. Seeing them approaching, Alicia moved away from the circle of friends that surrounded her.

Stepping to one side, Annias positioned himself so that he could carefully observe both people at the same time. Thaddaeus walked forward in a wooden but determined gait.

"Alicia," he bowed his head stiffly and his voice was flat.

Slowly she turned. Smiling faintly, Alicia simply acknowledged her name.

"I understand you wish to speak with me?"

"How have you been?" She seemed uncharacteristically unsteady and sounded vulnerable.

"I am fine," he stiffened. "You look well as always."

"I—I've been looking for you for a long time," she lowered her eyes. "Do you realize how long it has been since I've seen you—heard from you?"

Her question seemed to be an affront to the apostle. The sides of his face tightened and looked hard.

"What was it you wanted to ask me? You will appreciate how limited our time is."

"You have become an important person," her eyes searched his face, "and I am only an insignificant inquirer.

In this place I am nobody."

"Does Simeon know you are here?"

"Simeon?" Annias looked mystified. "Who is Simeon?"

"No." Alicia and Thaddaeus went on as if Annias had not spoken.

"Then *why* did you come?" The apostle's voice was increasingly hard and impersonal.

"I want to know more about all these things that you teach. I would like to understand what is going on in Jerusalem."

Thaddaeus blurted out, "I am well aware that Simeon does business with the Romans and is considered to be their confidant. Do you think I am deceived?" His eyes narrowed. "You have immediate access to the very people who keep us in bondage!"

"What are you suggesting?" Alicia's eyes flashed.

"Who could better inform anyone who wanted to persecute us than you?"

"How *dare* you accuse me of being a spy!" her black eyes snapped.

"Now, now," Annias interrupted, "this is not the way for us to find understanding." He reached for the arm of each person. "We are standing in the very room where the reconciliation of all humanity was proclaimed. Let us not quarrel. I know that both of you want only the best."

Although Thaddaeus drew his arm away, Alicia did not move. She breathed deeply and looked down at the floor.

"Please," Annias pleaded with the apostle, "please, hear her out."

"What do you want?" Thaddaeus finally asked.

"At first I came in curiosity," she shrugged. "Just after we moved to Jerusalem, the stories spread about Yeshua coming back to life. Of course, I don't believe in such things as a resurrection, but I was intrigued. I wondered what part you played in all of the strange things that were happening."

Annias motioned for Alicia to sit down on the bench by the large serving table. He tugged at Thaddaeus' sleeve.

"So," Alicia smiled again, "I have been coming to hear the teaching." She paused a moment and then added, "I came to scoff, but I have stayed to learn."

"And what have you learned?" Sitting down, Thaddaeus folded his arms across his chest.

"That I have been wrong about a great many things," she replied earnestly, "and that you can help me with many of my questions."

"I am nothing here—nothing more than anyone else. I am simply a servant of the Master." After a long pause he added, "But no one who comes in sincerity will ever be turned away."

"Good, good." Annias patted him on the back.

"Then," sudden intensity filled her voice, "I must know something that has haunted me for four years. Why does a man give up the whole world for a religious cause?"

"I did not follow a cause." He turned nervously in his chair. "I followed Yeshua."

"I cannot understand," she shook her head, "how in just one afternoon you could leave behind everything, *every-thing*, and go after Him."

Thaddaeus stood and started to turn away, but Annias pressed at his side. The apostle rubbed his temples with the palms of his hands and shifted his weight from one foot to the other.

"It is very difficult to explain such a thing," he began slowly, "but Yeshua put a claim on my life. I—I knew that I must follow wherever He went."

"A claim?" Alicia shook her head vigorously. "A claim? What does that mean? What could you find that was not already in our village?"

"Sometime in each of our lives," he slowly sought the right words, "a moment comes when we are confronted by the truth. At such a time we must decide where we will stand because the rest of life will be shaped and molded by what is chosen in that instant. That afternoon when the Rabbi stopped at the gate, He just looked at me. And, in His eyes I saw two things: the man I was and the man I could be." Thaddaeus watched her face carefully to see if she understood. "As Yeshua talked to me, He spoke to a hunger that churned in my soul. He told me how I could cross the chasm between what I am and what I ought to be."

For the first time Thaddaeus reached out to touch Alicia. "Forgive me that I never came back to explain. I know now that even my relentless pursuit of that vision was itself a reflection of my own willfulness."

Instantly she had withdrawn her hand and Annias realized that some enormous hidden piece of the conversation escaped him. He felt mystified by what he was witnessing.

"Never did He show me my limits without also revealing a love which completely accepted me," Thaddaeus' eyes searched hers, "and that has changed my life. When He called me, Yeshua said, 'I will give you a treasure that cannot be bought nor sold, an inheritance that can neither be earned nor taken away.' "

Alicia watched him with a look that was neither hostile nor pained. It was as if the words had been heard, but only as a mystery.

"I am still on the journey." Thaddaeus' gaze fell to the floor for a moment before he turned away from them. "I must be going," and he smiled kindly. "I hope this has helped." Before either could respond, he slipped behind the curtain, leaving them in the silent room.

CHAPTER THREE

TWILIGHT WAS FALLING when Annias stepped across the threshold into the inner courtyard of Simeon bar James. The spaciousness of the house bore ample witness to the wealth of its owner. The diplomat's trained eyes quickly assessed what he saw and measured its value. On every side there was ample opulence for him to consider. He mused that it would have been easier to follow Alicia to her house and gather information on her husband than it had been to finagle an invitation through his contacts to meet Simeon. However, when trade possibilities in Edessa had been mentioned to Simeon's colleagues, the invitation arrived quickly.

"Our house is honored by your presence." The servant bowed low. "I will inform my master of your arrival."

The old man studied the upper balcony that surrounded the courtyard. This was, indeed, a house of many rooms! In the courtyard's center was a large tree that gave its own testimony to the age of the house. Annias concluded that this was a most considerable estate for such a young man to possess.

"You have arrived. Welcome!" A handsome man swept across the stones with an easy regal bearing. "My house is most privileged to welcome the envoy of the King of Osrhoene."

"And I am honored by your hospitality," Annias bowed.

"I am Simeon," said the younger man extending his hand.

"Simeon bar James, your reputation has gone before you even into my country." Annias watched Simeon's face to see what response such flattery might have.

"Really!" Simeon beamed. "Well, I am delighted to hear it! Come into the house."

"He is young," Annias thought. "He mistakes a ploy for the truth!"

"Of course, we trade very extensively," Simeon continued as he quickly led them down one of the long halls, "but most of our interests do not usually take us that far away from Jerusalem. I am amazed you know of us." He moved abruptly leaving a hint of impetuosity. "Your king has sent you here to explore new trade routes?"

"We are always seeking new opportunities," Annias studied Simeon's large gold ring on his well-manicured hand. "New contacts are the lifeblood of business."

"Of course!" Simeon ushered him into a large dining hall. "You have come to a place where there are many open doors, and all of them receive you as an honored guest."

Annias was taken aback by the elaborate dinner prepared for him. The furnishings and tapestries of the room were more exquisite than any he had seen since coming to Jerusalem. Far from a simple supper, his host had spread a banquet before him.

"No expense is to be spared for our friends." Simeon gestured toward a silken couch as he took his own position. "To honor you is to honor your king."

Servants appeared with towels and basins and prepared

to wash Annias' feet. From another corner of the room, a dark-skinned woman brought in a golden kelix and poured him a cup of wine. Her eyes flashed their particular message of welcome and invitation.

"The first appearance is deceiving," Annias thought. "Such a youth is not to be underestimated. There is a cleverness here that must be carefully measured."

"But let us not talk of business," Simeon smiled, "when there is so much to be enjoyed. Who knows what pleasures the evening may yet bring." He looked knowingly at the servant girl who, in turn, bowed provocatively before Annias.

"Our friends lack for nothing when they visit us in Jerusalem." Simeon snapped his fingers and the array of foods increased as the servants brought in steaming dishes and platters of meat.

Following a toast, the banquet began. As they ate, Annias discovered that his new acquaintance moved the conversation easily and skillfully. He smiled realizing that information was being adroitly extracted from him amidst the many pleasantries. Remembering that his only reason for coming was to interrogate his host, Annias reflected that Simeon must not be allowed to turn the tables on him.

"Let me ask you something of your political situation," Annias said as he reached for a piece of mutton. "How does a Jerusalem Jew fare with the Romans who are both conquerors and masters of this land?"

"Why should you ask?" Simeon questioned his examiner.

"I too am a Jew," he smiled. "One who lives with a foreign ruler needs to acquire all the wisdom that the world offers."

Simeon's eyes narrowed as he paused. His reply came in measured tones, "Well, there are Jews and then there are Jews. I suppose one defines Jewishness by one's personal interest."

"M-m-m," Annias mused, "and how does one define such things in Jerusalem these days?"

"Some look for a Messiah while others find God in Torah. There are those who seek sport in trying to kill Romans. But the more prudent," Simeon chuckled, "pay attention to business and leave the gods and politics to the weak and foolish."

"What a fascinating man you are, Simeon! You have obviously learned how to wend your way through the streets of life as well as Jerusalem."

"I trust so," the younger man smiled warily.

"But the Romans," Annias leaned forward, "surely you must have some special relationship with them that allows your business to flourish here?"

"I am a Sadducee," Simeon said defensively. "This life is all I expect to get. So I handle it carefully, and avoid religion and politics in every way. I am a man of business, and the Romans like the way I do business. The matter is that simple."

"Oh," the older man dipped into the bowl before him "but surely you must be seen by them as a—shall we say a 'special friend'?"

Simeon leaned back on his couch carefully gauging the man before him. Finally he answered coldly, "I am not sure what you are asking. I drink with the Romans, I bribe the Romans, and I patronize them whenever business demands. However, I never put both feet into their world. Those who play such games of intrigue usually lose their toes."

Sensing a possible irritation, Annias chose his next words slowly. "Don't misunderstand me, my friend. As one who works for a king, I am always looking for ways to live in a world filled with Romans. After all, business is business. It simply occurred to me that one as ah, as important as yourself must be, on occasion, accommodating to the

Romans, ah, ah, should special needs arise."

"I do not collaborate." Simeon's voice took on an icy tone. "Business is business and no more than that."

"No offense, no offense!" Annias quickly held up his hand in an apologetic gesture. He knew he had found the boundaries he was seeking. "I meant nothing personal, only the usual interests of a diplomat." He smiled broadly to brake the rising tension. "Let me toast a most clever man of trade and a gracious host." The smile continued as he reached for his wine goblet. "To successful business!"

"Now I know," Annias thought to himself. "I have the answer I came for. This man is not likely to be a Roman collaborator."

"Tell me more of the commodities you seek." Simeon handed him a silver plate piled high with grapes as he moved the conversation in a direction more to his liking.

Annias countered with the doubletalk of a government official who seems to be saying one thing while meaning the opposite. His sweeping statements of new trade routes committed him to nothing and revealed little content.

After several minutes Annias felt ready to ask a question of his choosing. "Why is there such turmoil in Jerusalem? On every corner I hear of many strange religious ideas. This whole city seems to be in a continuous state of consternation. Everywhere I hear people speaking about a Messiah."

"People are crazy!" Simeon almost spit back into his goblet in disgust. "The fools babble incessantly about some messiah who will throw the Romans out. They refuse to recognize that Rome is today's god and that smart people will worship at that altar. Someday the Romans will go, but none of us will live to see it!"

"Yet, Simeon, others speak of another kind of Messiah. Can you tell me something about the one they called Yeshua?"

"His followers are the maddest of all! They are a disease

that has become the scourge of this city. You must be particularly careful of them, for their ideas spread like bad infection. Once people are touched by their visions, they even start seeing dead men walking around the streets!"

"Really?" Annias acted surprised. "What strange things do they teach?"

Simeon exploded with cynical laughter. Seizing his goblet, he gulped down more wine. For the first time, Annias realized that the younger man was drinking far too much.

"They say Yeshua did the greatest magic trick of all!" Simeon sneered. "These fanatics teach that their Master came back from the dead. In fact, they believe He still contacts them with special messages. Have you ever heard such madness?" Once again, he guzzled the wine.

"Yet," Annias bore down, "I hear nothing but good about these believers. Everywhere I turn I hear stories of their caring for the poor and the sick."

"The poor!" Simeon's voice rose to a shrill pitch. "Let them have the damned poor of this city, of this country, of the whole world! That's all they are good for! They and their Messiah know nothing about how this world must be run. They can rot with the poor, for all I care!" When he grabbed the goblet again, the wine ran down his beard.

Annias silently watched his host until the right question seemed to fall into his mind. "Did you ever meet this Yeshua?" he asked offhandedly.

"Did I ever meet Him?" Once more Simeon burst into cruel laughter and then abruptly became cold sober. "Yes— of course—I met Him."

"Interesting," Annias smiled. "I wondered if you might have. I hear so much about Him these days. Perhaps you could tell of your impression."

Simeon's lip curled. "A mad man! A source of confusion! He set brother against brother! Any sane person could quickly see through His pretense."

"You certainly have strong feelings about Him."

"No!" Simeon protested. "I care nothing about Him, nor the mad disciples who still follow His ghost!"

"Hm-mm." Annias smiled. "He seems to have certainly made an imprint on you."

Fire snapped in Simeon's eyes as he set his jaw tightly and defiantly. Quickly Annias again smiled kindly trying to imply only dispassioned interest. Slowly the younger man leaned back on his couch. "Yes, I met Him once. In fact, I talked with Him at some length."

Annias let silence be his persuader.

"Yes," Simeon began to reflect, "it was several years ago, in the north where I grew up. He came through our town and many went out to hear Him. In fact, my whole family was much taken when He talked. After all, the rumor was spreading that He might be the new David who would free us from the Romans."

"What did He teach, Simeon?"

"Much to my surprise, He would not talk of wars or politics. Rather, He said that we must be willing to carry even the crushing weight of injustice in order to accomplish the purposes of love. The kingdom He taught was one in which everyone simply followed the will of God."

"Well," the old man laughed, "how could anyone be offended by such a message?"

"His words flowed like a river," Simeon's voice softened, "but always there was another hidden river that was deeper down, like an underground stream. His ideas had many layers and in the end you discovered that He was asking more of you than appeared when He began. Many of His teachings sounded very simple unless one tried to live them. This Yeshua always fished with a hidden hook."

"And what happened to you?" Annias leaned forward. "Did that hook snag you?"

A troubled look glazed the young man's eyes. A look of

unexpected vulnerability and honesty settled on his face as his recollections came back into clear focus. "One afternoon I went out to meet Him at the city gate. I asked Him the one question that puzzles every Sadducee: Is there an afterlife, an eternal life, a resurrection?

"His countenance conveyed an invitation to approach Him and at first He seemed very gentle. But there was nothing weak about Him. In fact, I felt almost intimidated by the power that came from His personality. There was a strange contradiction in Him that both drew me and held me back. I suppose I was amazed that someone who did not have money or power, and who wanted neither, could command such respect from me.

"So I asked Him, 'Rabbi, what must I do to inherit eternal life?' I thought an answer to this question would clarify everything! If I could believe that there was more than only this life, I would change everything I did. Of course, I was intrigued about such a matter."

"And how did He answer you?" Annias felt himself straining forward to catch every word.

"At first He turned the question aside. Instead, He asked me about my life. As any good rabbi would do, He questioned me about keeping the law. Had I kept the commandments? Did I supremely love God?"

"And had you? Did you?" Annias pursued.

"Of course! The family of bar James always kept the law! We observed the rituals; my father taught us the rules." Defensiveness had returned to Simeon's voice. "No one is perfect, but we did not steal or kill. I was completely respectable," he stopped and added, "then."

"So?" Annias persisted.

"I never thought of our religion as anything other than rules to be kept. We were Jews because this is what Jews do. It was as simple as that!" Contempt began to settle on Simeon's face as he seemed to be directing his conversation elsewhere. "Isn't it enough to be decent people who intend no harm? What is wrong with prospering and accumulating? Why should the strong not dominate the weak? Well, apparently none of this was good enough for Yeshua. He swept all of my goodness aside as too elementary to be considered. Obeying the law was not enough to satisfy His appetite! He said I must love everyone as God loves, if life was to stay in me."

"My friend," Annias reached over in a reassuring gesture, "this Yeshua has made you very angry."

"Angry?" Simeon puzzled over the word. "Perhaps, but that doesn't quite touch the center. Yeshua wanted to make God into an all-consuming fire! He would have reduced all of my dreams and hopes to ashes. No, not anger; He made me afraid. If I had done what He asked, I would have lost myself and been consumed by this all-passionate love of God which He taught."

Silence fell between the two men. Simeon stared at the bowl until the silence no longer was endurable. "He wanted me to give up all my power and take care of the poor! I was to release my servants and become a servant to everyone else. If I did that, then I could return and be His follower. If I gave my life away, I would have it forever!"

"And that made you angry?" Annias asked again.

"Perhaps that is the strangest effect of all. Yeshua could do unusual things with people's minds. No, I was not angry. I wanted to do it. At that moment the most wonderful vision passed across my mind. I saw myself as a bird that soared up to the heights of heaven and flew unencumbered over the whole of creation. An intoxicating liberation filled me and I felt as though I could shed every weight. Angry? No, far from it! I wanted to do exactly what He said."

The light of the flickering torches danced in Simeon's eyes. Annias realized they were burning low as the whole room was becoming a place of shadows.

"And you said no?"

The young man nodded his head in confirmation.

"An old man knows how all of life is shaped by such moments. The yes or the no changes everything."

"Of course I said no!" Simeon snapped. "It was all a moment of madness spun by a village preacher. Fools followed Him; men of discernment took another road!"

Simeon suddenly stood up and shook his robes as if to shake away the moment. "We cannot talk in such darkness," he grumbled. "The twilight plays tricks on us. I'll have the fire in the lamps built up." His abrupt handclap echoed down the halls. "Where are those worthless servants?"

The old man heard feet scurrying behind him. Yet the lightness of the step was different from the servant's who had been there earlier in the evening.

"Light!" Simeon growled. "Bring us more oil!"

"The servants are not here." A familiar voice answered from the hallway.

Simeon began a curse, then changed his tone. "Here is someone you must meet! My wife is the delight of my house."

Annias turned to find Alicia standing behind him. Her black eyes registered shock and alarm; yet without changing expression, she lowered her head in acknowledgment of his presence.

"We have an important guest, my dear. May I introduce Annias who comes as the envoy of the king of Osrhoene. He brings us exciting news!"

As Annias bowed, he tried to appear kind and reassuring so that Alicia would know she had nothing to fear. In turn, her stare was intense and threatening.

"And what is this unusual message that such a distinguished visitor might tell us?" Her tight-lipped smile barely concealed her anger.

"He brings us news of business, of course! My reputation has spread to the far corners of the world. Even now, the king of his great country wishes to trade with me!"

"Oh?" Alicia's voice was cool. "How very unexpected."

"Not at all!" Simeon sounded slightly annoyed. "You must learn to expect such things. Our businesses are expanding all the time."

"So, the envoy of the great king of Osrhoene has come here to Jerusalem on business?" Alicia continued to watch the old man's eyes intensely. "And you have no other interests but business?"

"I handle many matters for my king." Annias again smiled reassuringly. "I am his trusted servant who keeps secrets well. So I explore a wide range of concerns."

"Yes, yes," Simeon sounded more irritated. "We still have much to discuss! Where are those worthless servants? The lights are getting dim."

When Simeon stepped into the hall to call for the servants again, Alicia moved closer to Annias and said in a low voice, "My, but it is a surprise to see you here." Her sweetness was saccharine and cynical. "Isn't it a coincidence that you should turn up in *my* house?"

"Our paths do seem to cross in the most unexpected ways." Once more Annias tried to smile disarmingly.

"My husband thinks of business and little else. I hope you can appreciate this limitation."

"Tonight has helped me understand more than you might expect. Alicia, I assure you that you have nothing to fear from my conversation."

"Some things are best not tampered with," Alicia warned. "There are doors to be opened and others to be left closed. I trust you can discern the difference."

"Of course, of course," Annias kept smiling.

The sound of feet approaching in the corridor ended the quiet exchange. One servant quickly began to trim the wicks as another poured oil into the lamps.

"Well," Simeon laughed nervously, "at least the slothfulness of my servants has given you time to get acquainted." Looking proudly at his wife, he smiled. "Annias, you can see that my taste in all things is impeccable."

Alicia lowered her gaze to the floor.

"Indeed!" Annias acknowledged. "Your wife is a woman of great mystery."

"Mystery?" Simeon chuckled. "Mystery? Ah, you diplomats are adroit with your words. Alicia, who would have thought of you as a woman of intrigue?"

Alicia continued looking silently at the floor.

"Now this is a rare moment!" Simeon chided his wife. "My wife is speechless!"

"I think it is time for me to retire," Annias nodded to both of them. "The evening is getting late."

"Oh, no!" Simeon protested. "We have not settled and—ah—er—well, we still have much left to discuss. We have not signed any trade agreements. Please stay the night with us. I have already made the preparations."

"You are most gracious, but I have pressing business rather early in the morning."

As if on cue, the alluring woman servant stepped out of the shadows. "Would my lord care for more refreshment?" her smile was seductive.

"Oh, but you must stay the night with us!" Simeon insisted.

Alicia said nothing, but she scrutinized Annias intensely.

"We have made a good beginning," the diplomat said firmly. "We have an excellent basis for our further discussions, so we can easily proceed later. I must be leaving."

"Perhaps," Simeon insisted, "in the morning we could talk in detail of the trade routes to the north."

Annias bowed and said, "You will be hearing from me, Simeon. Thank you for a delightful evening."

"But," the host pursued, "I don't know where to contact you."

The old man kept moving toward the outer door. "I am sure you can appreciate my need for security. I will call you."

"Security?" Simeon puzzled. "Is Jerusalem such a dangerous city?"

"Security is important to a diplomat." Annias kept walking. Turning to Alicia, "And I will be looking forward to seeing your wife again."

"Of course," she acknowledged, "the pleasure will be mine."

Before Simeon could protest further, Annias had moved into the courtyard and was on his way to the outer gate. Almost before the servant had reached the door, he was gone.

"I don't understand this," Simeon stared in consternation. "We hardly completed our business!"

"Maybe he finished his business," Alicia said coldly.

"What do you mean?"

"Obviously, this man is not some simple trader from Jericho, Simeon. Possibly he had intentions he didn't reveal."

"Do you think I am a fool, woman? Can you negotiate business better than I? I would have recognized such a hidden purpose!"

"Of course," she conceded. As she observed the woman of convenience still standing behind them, she added, "You are a man of great subtleties."

Eyeing the woman, Simeon retorted, "One does what is necessary. Men understand what women cannot fathom."

"Of course," and her disgust was evident. "I am going to bed."

Simeon watched her cross the open courtyard. He started to answer her with a parting taunt, but thought the better of it. Irritation and frustration had begun to creep over him. Simeon did not like the feeling that he was not in complete control, or one step behind any opponent. And yet, he sensed that the evening was now in some way strangely out of focus. For a moment he looked at the star-filled sky. It seemed empty and very distant. "Business and money," he said aloud, "make *this* world run."

CHAPTER FOUR

THE ROOM WAS already crowded when Alicia made her way down the stairs. Her eyes darted from group to group, since she knew Annias would be at the center of one of the discussions. Finally she spotted him near the front of the room.

"If you please—" she stepped into the group. "Might I speak with you in private?"

Annias turned to find the small woman directly in front of him. Alicia abruptly stepped away from the group and gave Annias no alternative but to go to her. She turned her back to the gathering forcing him to look her full in the face.

"I trust you found what you were looking for!" Her eyes snapped.

"Please, you must understand." He extended his hands to her.

"And were you able to uncover any secrets at my house?" Alicia ignored his apologetic tone.

"Please," Annias pleaded, "surely you realize that I do business for my king."

"Business? Really!" Alicia contradicted him. "You came for nothing more than to see if I am a spy, a traitor!"

"Please, please," Annias tried to lower his voice, "this is all a misunderstanding."

"There is no misunderstanding!" Alicia's voice became very intense. "You wanted to trick me!"

Fearing that people might turn to listen to their conversation, Annias tried to move her farther back from the crowd. Alicia shrugged off his hand.

"Forgive me," Annias begged in exasperation. "Surely you can appreciate how sensitive all of these matters are. It was important for me to know the truth."

"And now you know?" Alicia questioned haughtily.

"Of course!" the diplomat recovered his steadiness. "All questions have been answered. Rest assured I harbor no suspicions. I accuse you of nothing!"

She whirled away. After a step she stopped. "Well," she said slowly, "if you are sincere, you can make amends by convincing the apostle that I am not a spy."

"Certainly, certainly," Annias quickly agreed.

"My friends," the leader called over the noise of conversations, "it is time to begin." The man silenced the room with, "Let us pray."

Men and women moved into separate groups. Some knelt on the floor, others leaned against the walls, while a few sat on the benches. Annias blended into the kneeling crowd. Prayer began spontaneously and fervently all over the room. Alicia too slipped down to the floor. A spirit of adoration swept over the assembly as the intensity of their praise filled the air.

Alicia felt the effect of their fervor although she could not understand it. As the prayers around her rose in crescendos, her mind wandered in other directions. She had never thought to doubt Thaddaeus when he told her about the details of his personal encounter with Yeshua. While she could not fully understand the whole account, the story had left its impact. She certainly was no longer able to dismiss these people of the Way as fanatics and fools, but she pondered what had really changed the apostle's heart.

As the spontaneous prayers ended, the big leader they called Simon lifted his hand. "Let us sing of the glory of God's victory. 'Though He was in the form of God,' " his deep voice soared in song, " 'He did not consider equality to be grasped.' "

The rest of the voices picked up the hymn, "but emptied Himself taking the form of a servant." Once again the fervor of devotion filled the room as the chant continued, "being born in the likeness of men, He humbled Himself and became obedient unto death, even death on a cross."

Since the hymn was unfamiliar to Alicia, she could only listen. The paradoxes puzzled her and the message seemed beyond her grasp.

When the anthem concluded, the leader began to teach. "As we live the life of faith, we see how weakness is strength. We empty ourselves in order to be filled with Him."

Even though Alicia heard every word, she could not make the meanings fit. If the leader was right, her world was totally wrong. She felt as if she had come to a wall that could not be penetrated. Her curiosity was turning into honesty and self-condemnation. No longer did she feel superior to those around her.

When the teaching was finished and the last prayer said, Alicia found Annias again. "There is a question that I must ask Thaddaeus. Would you please help me?"

"Of course." The old man seemed relieved to no longer be under attack. "But we must move quickly, since he leaves when the meetings are over."

She could see Thaddaeus at the back of the hall near the curtain that covered the hidden exit. A young man was asking him questions. Quietly but quickly Alicia moved between him and the curtain.

"—and so we must believe." Thaddaeus finished and turned toward the curtain.

"We have a question," Annias quickly interjected.

The apostle's eyes darted back and forth nervously. "Yes?" He answered hesitantly.

"I still do not understand this faith of yours," Alicia smiled in a shy way. "What *did* make you believe? Why do you have faith in Him?"

"Feel free to speak your mind," Annias begged. "Your words are safe with us."

Thaddaeus' eyes moved across her face and then fixed on Annias. "You are asking about faith? You want to know why a person believes?"

"No," Alicia tried to sound sincere. "I want to know why *you* believe."

"Faith is like a tiny mustard seed," Thaddaeus explained. "Once the seed is planted, growth follows naturally."

"I don't understand how it is first planted," Alicia interrupted, trying to look into Thaddaeus' eyes. "How did growth begin in you?"

Thaddaeus seemed distracted. He was clearly avoiding looking into her eyes. "The starting place is to believe in the Person. Until we believe in Him, the seed has not been planted."

"Um-m," Annias mused in reflection for a moment.

Alicia moved closer. "How do *I* start believing in someone whom I have not seen?"

Thaddaeus stepped back from her and looked toward Annias. "Faith is always a gift, Alicia. You must receive the seed by asking Him to plant it in your heart."

"Yes!" Annias exclaimed with understanding. "One must *want* to believe and then ask for help to believe even more."

"Exactly!" Thaddaeus nodded. "Some receive the gift

before they even know they are asking, while others must make a long journey to find the same answer."

"Do you really want this gift?" Annias said, turning to Alicia. "What if God planted such a seed in your life? Do you realize what such a faith might become? A mustard tree grows to an awesome size."

Alicia turned toward one of the benches. Feeling the rough edges, she contrasted for an instant the barrenness of the poorly furnished room with the lavishness of her own home. "I suppose that knowing what I want is the crucial question," she concluded, with her back to both men. "I'm not sure that I know what it is I am really seeking."

Annias walked toward her, but after an awkward silence turned back toward the apostle. The swinging curtain was the only trace of Thaddaeus' departure.

"He's gone!" Annias exclaimed in consternation.

"Oh, yes," Alicia sighed, "Thaddaeus is trying to drive me away. I think he fears me even more than you do."

"Please! Please!" Annias protested. "That is all past. I am going to talk to him about this ridiculous situation right now!"

The old man bolted for the curtain. "When I see you tomorrow, I know matters will be different!"

The diplomat almost slipped and fell as he skipped steps in his haste to catch up with the apostle. He ran through the door and out into the street. Thaddaeus was just about to turn the corner onto another street when Annias saw him and dashed down the narrow alley.

"Stop!" he shouted, "Stop up there!"

Thaddaeus turned to see where the commotion was coming from and realized who was pursuing him.

"Wait a minute!" the old man puffed as he caught up with him. "You're not going to run away from this today. We are going to talk about this situation whether you like it or not"

"Situation?" Thaddaeus acted puzzled. "I don't know what you mean."

"Listen!" the old man shook his finger in the apostle's face, "I know this woman is not a spy! I have been to her house and I have even met her husband. And—"

"You did what?" Thaddaeus exploded. "You met her husband?"

"Exactly!" Annias stood his ground. "And I know they are not spies."

"How dare you meddle in other people's affairs!" The apostle's eyes blazed. "Who asked you to stick your nose in places it does not belong?"

"I will not be intimidated by you," Annias fired back. "I know all about Alicia and her husband and—"

"You are a fool!" Thaddaeus cut him off. "You know nothing about this woman and her husband!"

"A fool?" Annias gasped. "A fool?" His voice dropped. "Did not Yeshua once say that anyone who calls his brother a fool is himself in danger of judgment?"

Thaddaeus clenched his jaw tightly. "Let me assure you, old man, that you have not begun to know this woman and her husband. You have been deceived by appearances."

"Her husband's only interest is business," Annias again shook his finger at the apostle. "I say that he is not our enemy!"

Thaddaeus stared hard at Annias as he carefully measured his words. "Her—husband—is—my—brother."

"What?" the diplomat's jaw dropped.

"Simeon is my younger brother."

"Your brother?"

"Do not tell me again you know all about this family."

"Oh, no!" Annias gasped. "I had no idea—"

"Exactly! Your hand is on a hot poker and you stand on the edge of fire. You are walking on a path of which you know nothing. Measure your steps well, lest you slip!"

With that, the apostle turned into the passing crowd and disappeared onto another street.

"His brother!" Annias gasped in astonishment. For a long time he stood on the corner trying to fit the pieces of the puzzle together.

That night Alicia was more subdued than usual as she dined with her husband. Reclining on couches, their conversation was aimless and banal. Though the dining room was more comfortable and luxurious than her surroundings of a few hours earlier, it felt lifeless and cold to her.

Throughout the meal she had taken full measure of Simeon. Although smaller and less muscular than Thaddaeus, he had the same handsomeness, and bore a definite resemblance to his brother. Alicia realized for the first time how often she had fought back any comparison of the two. Yet, the plainness of the apostle's robe and the purple trimmed toga of the businessman made their own stark contrast. Simeon cherished the ways of luxury and had little trouble in adjusting to the Roman conquerors. He was a man skilled in compromise.

The three years of their marriage kept running through her mind. Simeon's abilities had swept her from the most remote world of Caesarea by the Sea to the center of power in Jerusalem. While most of the girls of her village had married earlier, she had waited until she was seventeen to make sure she found the husband of her choosing. "How ironic," she thought, "for one accustomed to getting her way! This is what I have ended up with!"

"You are a most remarkable woman," Simeon remarked, as he reached for the golden wine cup.

"Oh?" she smiled. "Why would you say that?"

"I am married to the most beautiful woman in all of Jerusalem and yet none of my friends see you anymore."

She knew he liked the way the Romans turned their heads to watch her. In fact, he encouraged her to be enticing. The disdain of the Jewish women toward Alicia's seductive adornment only amused him further. Simeon wanted his wife to be a trophy that was seen and coveted.

"Well," she bantered, "is that not an insurance of my virtue?"

"Indeed so!" he chuckled. "But what do you do with your time? You have servants to care for your every need."

"Perhaps I pray at the temple," she said coolly, as she poured more wine into his cup.

"What a sense of humor you have," he laughed. "You are always amusing and I like that. You have the style of the women of Rome."

"And you have the sensitivity of an ox," she thought. Silently she realized that his compliments indicted her for immodesty.

"Is my praying so amusing?" she asked seriously. "Perhaps I am capable only of amusing you."

"Ah, now you have become the woman of mystery!" he laughed again. "I know better than to believe you would indulge in religious nonsense."

"Are we not still Jews who look for a Messiah?" she showed her irritation.

"The only messiah I look for is the one I put in my treasure chest."

Alicia despised Simeon's condescending air. Though her face did not reflect any emotion, she felt angry as she contrasted the arrogance of his greed with the unassuming benevolence of his brother.

"Simeon, do you ever give any thought to religious matters?"

"Of course not! I leave that foolishness for my half-witted brother."

Alicia's face flushed. The mere mention of Thaddaeus

had always caused a tension between them, but never had her hostility been so intense. "Have you ever considered what he is doing and why he has continued to live the life he does?" She tried to sound detached.

"Never!" Simeon said defiantly.

"Did you know that he is here in Jerusalem?"

"Certainly!" Simeon said contemptuously. "Who can escape these ridiculous stories that he and his moon-touched friends keep spreading. They do nothing but stir up trouble among our people and with the Romans."

"Still, their movement seems to be growing quite rapidly," Alicia observed quietly.

"Good heavens!" Simeon exploded. "In my own house I hear this rubbish! Just the mention of Thaddaeus and his Messiah-madness ruins the supper!"

He abruptly pushed back from the couch and stood up. As he left from the room, he turned and muttered sarcastically, "I trust you will find something better to do with your time than to listen to the superstitious tales of idle women and degenerate men!"

As the servant girl began to clear the table, Alicia stared at her plate in painful silence. She knew better than to speak back to Simeon. But the longer she sat in silence, the more contemptuous of him she felt.

Alicia's gaze fell on her polished wine cup. In its mirror-like finish, her darkly lined eyes formed a strange, blurry pattern. As she tilted her head, the design moved slowly, like a reflection in a pond. As Alicia studied her carefully contoured eyes, she began to realize that in only a few years, the innocence of her youth had disappeared beneath the layers of accommodation to the demands of prestige. Now Alicia saw the image of a woman of the world who had learned to practice the art of deception.

Alicia blinked abruptly at the realization of her insight. Someone whom she hardly knew and completely disliked had appeared before her in the reflection. Slowly and subtly, the simple village girl had become a sophisticate of the city. She was Alicia, wife of Simeon, a woman who had learned how to court the wealthy and powerful.

The metal mirror told her another truth—that Simeon was a disappointment to her. He was cold, indifferent, and calculating; yet, she had learned to enjoy the harvest that his callousness brought to their table. What she resented most was her own compromise with the evils of power. No one had forced her to choose the ways of expediency. She recognized that her contempt for Simeon arose from a disdain for what she herself had become. The sting of her lost innocence touched her very soul.

A vision of the simple plainness of her mother floated before Alicia's eyes. She remembered the virtues and ideals of a good Jewish woman. Goodness wrapped itself around her mother like a well-fashioned garment. Alicia's parents had always been devout Jews who kept the Sabbath and never deviated from the law of Moses. Although poor, they had never been impoverished. Only now did she feel truly indigent.

The wealth of Simeon's family had been an enticement to another way of life. The bar James were the elite power brokers of the province and enjoyed the favor of the tax collectors and soldiers. Caesarea had been just enough of a crossroads with the world to whet her appetite for the finest and the best.

Thaddaeus had once offered her this prestige, but also a continuation of a cherished way of life. She would have needed to make only a small step to obtain his level of influence.

On the other hand, marrying Simeon demanded a great leap into a realm where the traditions of common villagers were despised. Simeon knew so well how to spin his own webs of intrigue. Alicia realized that he had also spun a cocoon from which her own metamorphosis had sprung. Life with Simeon had changed her into another person. She too had become a schemer, crafty and designing.

The truth became painfully clear—she had had so much ambition that she did not resist. When Thaddaeus had left, she felt strangely cut loose from the moorings of her childhood. Then she decided Simeon's road to power would also be the path to happiness. But now, she was no longer sure of what was important and valuable.

Looking around at all the symbols of their success, Alicia felt an emptiness welling up inside of her. She had left behind the only treasure worth having and had sold her birthright to the low bidder.

"I have become a slave in my own world, a prisoner in my own jail," she said dryly, to no one in particular.

The startled servant stopped her cleaning and stared at her.

"I must find an inheritance that cannot be earned," she went on, "a treasure that cannot be bought if I am to have a life worth living." She pushed back from the table and walked slowly toward her bedroom.

The next morning Annias waited for the upper room to clear after the teaching time before approaching Thaddaeus. Both men were aware that Alicia had not been there.

"Surely you know," Annias began apologetically, "that I intended no offense. I have not meant to go where I did not belong."

Thaddaeus nodded. "There should be no harsh word between brothers." He smiled weakly. "Let us consider the matter closed."

"Certainly," the old man said quietly, "and yet, I must inquire a bit further."

When Thaddaeus said nothing, Annias nervously shifted

his weight. "I talked with your brother about possible trade agreements. I am sure he thought of me only as an envoy of my king, yet during the conversation he also spoke of his own confrontation with the Messiah."

Again, the apostle only nodded.

"Nothing that I have seen condemns the woman," Annias finally said in exasperation. "Surely you cannot reject her because your brother refused to follow!"

Thaddaeus sighed deeply and his eyes dropped to the ground. More than hesitant, he seemed sad and his words sounded heavy. "All right, I will tell you the whole story. I am sure you will appreciate my desire for confidentiality."

"Of course! Of course!"

"Four years ago, Yeshua came through our village. My brother and I were sitting by the gate when He entered. He called us to follow Him. When I saw Him, I was compelled to draw close and to listen."

"And your brother?"

"It was the same with Simeon. He also knew that he was to follow Him."

"And your family? How did they feel about this young Rabbi and His call?"

"Our family have always been Sadducees with great wealth and holdings. It was not easy to tolerate someone who talked of caring for the poor and giving away possessions. As the eldest, I was soon to become responsible for the family fortune."

"Oh!" Annias' eyes widened as his hand came to his mouth. The old man dropped down on the bench behind him. "When you followed Yeshua, you gave up your inheritance?"

Thaddaeus shrugged.

"Your brother has such wealth because he received your portion?"

"I heeded the call to follow the Master and left everything

70

behind. It has all become Simeon's."

"Good heavens! You *did* leave everything behind!"

"My family renounced me, and Simeon gladly took my place."

"Then why should he wish you any harm? Surely he has nothing to fear from you?"

"You must remember that no one could be confronted by Yeshua and remain the same. He might be denied, but never ignored."

"Ah, your decision to follow doubly condemns your brother!"

"Apparently he thinks so," the apostle smiled sadly, "though nothing condemns him but his own conscience."

"But such difficulties can be clarified—" the diplomat reasoned.

"No!" Thaddaeus interrupted him. "When Yeshua was crucified, Simeon felt completely vindicated. Remember, Sadducees don't believe in resurrection."

Annias stroked his beard, pondering the amazing story. "And the woman?" he finally ventured. "What part does she play in all of this?"

"Alicia was betrothed to me before I left to follow the Master," Thaddaeus said softly. "We would have been married if I had stayed at home."

"Oh, no!" Annias gasped. "I had no idea!"

"Now you understand. No one else knows of this—you can see why I have avoided her."

Dumbfounded, Annias only shook his head.

"I am not sure of her reasons, Annias. Of course, she never saw Yeshua, and what she knows of my motives is mainly what Simeon told her. Perhaps her interest is genuine, but I am hesitant. She will have to prove herself to me." Thaddaeus turned and walked toward the curtain. "I appreciate your concern," he said, parting the curtain, "but these matters must be left in God's hands."

Annias did not try to follow him down the back stairway. The old man continued to sit on the bench and shake his head. Finally he concluded, "The ways of God are indeed passing strange!"

Alicia waited two days before going to the apostle's house. Only the inner circle of believers knew where Thaddaeus lived and it had not been easy to get the directions from Annias. She had even avoided the morning teaching times in order to be clear about her own purposes and to recover something of her lost sense of honesty. Only after she had become certain of her own intentions did she begin her journey to the unmarked door that opened into the apostle's residence.

"What do you want?" came from behind the old wooden door.

"I am only seeking the Way," she answered softly. She had been told that this phrase always gained entry.

The door cracked slightly and she saw the outline of a young man. Since she was alone, the hidden figure opened the door wider to let her slide through.

"I have come to talk with Thaddaeus. We have spoken together before."

"Please wait," a young man instructed her. Through the crack she could see him cross the small open courtyard and disappear into the house. Quickly he reappeared and allowed her to enter.

Although it was still early in the afternoon, the room was dim and filled with shadows. Five men were seated around a table and Thaddaeus stood at the far end of the room next to another doorway.

"Peace be unto you," one of the men greeted her. "How may we help you?"

"I need to speak with Thaddaeus."

"He is just leaving," the man continued. "Perhaps we can be of assistance."

Alicia fixed her eyes on Thaddaeus and tried silently to convey her sincerity. Then she said, "Please, Thaddaeus, I must speak with you alone."

The men exchanged sober glances and then looked to Thaddaeus.

"These are my true brothers," he began. "Please meet Andrew, James, Matthew, Joseph whom we have surnamed Barnabas, and Thomas. Nothing is hidden among us."

Each man nodded and smiled cordially. Alicia moved closer to the table and toward Thaddaeus.

"I know it is unusual for me to meet with the apostle alone and I do not wish to cause any interruption or problem," she stated carefully. "However, I have been trying to understand the faith you proclaim and I need Thaddaeus' help in knowing how I can believe in your Messiah. I knew the apostle many years ago in our village."

A murmur of appreciation and approval went around the room. The men nodded to Thaddaeus as if to say that they felt the need was genuine.

"We will leave you to discuss these matters alone," Matthew said.

As they began leaving, Alicia sat down at the table. The light coming through the small windows settled around her. Quietly she waited for Thaddaeus to acknowledge her.

"You seem so different today," Thaddaeus finally responded.

"I am different." She felt her cheek remembering that all makeup was gone and only her natural appearance remained.

Thaddaeus frowned and pursed his lips. His eyes darted away as if he didn't want to look too long. "What more can I say?" he finally offered.

"I'm not sure," she began falteringly, "but I believe you hold the key to what I need to know. I must hear what only you can tell me."

She knew that her coquettishness was gone and there were no hidden messages in her eyes. Her whole manner was straightforward and honest. "When I first came to the group, I was only seeking a diversion. I wanted to satisfy my curiosity. Perhaps I would see that you were really mad or—" Alicia stopped and then said slowly, "that perhaps you had found some other woman. I am still confused about what I wanted."

Thaddaeus sat down slowly.

"I can't tell you when I began to change," she said, lowering her gaze, "but as I listened, the words cast a strange spell over me. I was drawn to something I neither believed nor wanted. I do not understand what happened."

"That is the way it always is," the apostle said thoughtfully. "All of us are drawn by a power greater than ourselves. We seek to understand, only to discover that we are already understood."

"Your very words are a mystery," she protested. "I don't know what you mean when you talk like that. All of you seem to have a secret and I don't know how to find it. When you talked of Yeshua calling you, something began to work in my mind. You said that He made you see what you were and what you could be."

"Yes, He did!"

"Well, your teachings showed me both what I used to be and what I have become," she said painfully. "I pray to God you can tell me how He caused you to become what you are."

"I'm not sure of what I ought to say," he spoke haltingly. "What He gives is always a gift."

"If you could give me something I could see or touch—I

need a key to fit the lock that is wrapped inside this mystery."

"Remember," Thaddaeus replied, "many who saw the Master still rejected Him. The answer you seek is always a matter of faith. You cannot prove that He is the Way."

"You don't understand," Alicia said, as she felt her frustration increasing. "I feel as though I have been pushed out into a foggy swamp; I want you to show me a few stepping-stones."

"The path you seek is inside your heart, Alicia. Only *you* can make the decisions that will lead you to the answers you want."

Both felt an impasse had been reached and neither knew which way to turn. Alicia could not go backward or forward, and Thaddaeus had no other explanations. She stared out of the window as Thaddaeus sat silently.

"I remember something!" she said abruptly. "Annias spoke of the strange effect on him of a cloth which had touched His body. He spoke of a confirmation of his hopes."

"Do you mean the burial shroud of Yeshua?" Thaddaeus' brow wrinkled.

"I think so. He spoke of a cloth with a picture."

"We do not preach superstitious nonsense!" he said disdainfully.

"Perhaps something from *Him* would help me to believe."

"I find that suggestion distasteful," Thaddaeus was abrupt. "We are not magicians with cheap tricks."

"Please, don't be angry with me, Thaddaeus. I am floundering and I have no one to guide me. Can you deny me something to help me find my way?"

"There is no special power in the linen," he protested. "It is only a stained reminder of the glorious victory of the Lord."

"Then why should you deny me the opportunity of seeing it? Can it hurt anything?"

"What would people think if they knew I was causing you to handle objects defiled by death?" he protested. "The fellowship would be scandalized!"

"As a Sadducee, I do not worry about such matters. I promise I will tell no one, Thaddaeus. Please, just let me see it."

He rubbed his forehead wearily, then finally got up from the table. Thaddaeus looked at her as if to protest one more time and then gazed out the window for a few moments. With a sigh, he turned to a chest hidden in a shadowed corner. Carefully raising the lid, he lifted the package that was tied just as it had been when he received it from Joanna. Once the bundle was opened on the table, Thaddaeus stepped back.

"You will see that there is nothing special here."

"Perhaps," she slowly moved toward the cloth, "will you let me sit here quietly and try to consider what all of this means. We have just never believed in any resurrection."

Alicia reached out to open the folded sheet. As the first layer turned back, she saw the faint outline which revealed a face. The silhouette jolted her. Alicia had not expected what she was seeing—a complete face. She stared incredulously at the shroud. Thaddaeus turned and went out of the room, leaving her to her own meditations.

The shadows had lengthened into night when Thaddaeus finally returned. He found that the shroud was inside its covering and Alicia was gone. He had to light a candle to put the shroud back into the chest. Long into the night he pondered their conversation and wondered what he should have said to better answer her questions.

The next morning it was earlier than usual when Thaddaeus

entered the upper room to prepare for the daily meeting. Much to his surprise he found Alicia already there, seated on the floor. She was wearing the same plain robe from the day before.

"I believe," she said quietly.

"What?"

"I believe," she again said simply.

"I don't understand—"

"I know that He lives."

"What are you saying to me?" he asked, more in consternation than doubt. "What do you mean?"

"Last night I found my way. I prayed."

"And—?" Thaddaeus asked, dumbfounded.

"And I asked Him to do with me as He had done with others. I laid my life open before Him."

Thaddaeus knew all of these words, for he had heard them many times from others during the past months. Yet he could not believe his ears; her experience completely contradicted his convictions.

Thaddaeus could only stare at her. The room was filling and the intimacy of their conversation would soon be lost. Yet he could not answer.

"I want no more than to be one of His followers." Alicia raised her eyes to look deeply in his.

Thaddaeus saw that her face had truly changed. The day before, she had looked as if she had returned to the ways of the village; today a deeper, more inner transformation seemed evident. Thaddaeus could not deny what he saw before him.

The sudden silence in the room jolted him. Looking around he saw people watching him. Aware of their expectation, he moved to the head table where the teaching was always given. The room was crowded and the other leaders were seated at their places around the room. Annias had taken his usual seat from which he could observe every movement in the group.

"Yeshua said, 'If any man would come after Me,' Thaddaeus seemed to be struggling to find the right words, 'let him take up his cross and follow Me.'"

Sitting with her bowed head covered, Alicia seemed to be looking humbly at the floor. Her change was so profound that Thaddaeus felt confused.

"And Yeshua also said, 'My burden is light and My yoke is easy.'"

His mind drifted back to a scene two years earlier on the road to Jericho. A blind man had called out to Yeshua and his sight was restored. Thaddaeus had not then been able to comprehend what had really happened. But now he knew.

"We must all struggle with the meaning of the mystery of our faith." His words were disjointed from his thoughts. Even though he continued to instruct, he felt adrift in a sea of his own words.

CHAPTER FIVE

The cool breezes of late afternoon swept through the tall stone columns along the roofline of the temple portico. The lofty shelter of the portico offered temple worshipers a panoramic view of the green, rolling mountainsides surrounding Jerusalem. From the south end of the pinnacle, they could see passes opening into valleys that led down to the Dead Sea. As the sun's setting left its lingering glow, a hush descended on the ancient city of prayer.

One of the worshipers, Annias, sat transfixed by what he was hearing, set as it was in the peaceful twilight. Although he had been in meetings with John called the Beloved, he had not heard him teach before today. As John spoke beneath the high spans of the portico, Annias was touched by the compassionate quality of his message. Even John Mark, who had accompanied him, was unusually attentive. Having called for the brothers to love everyone, John finished with a prayer.

As the shadows lengthened and the crowd diminished, Annias, John, and John Mark descended the massive stone steps which led from the temple mount through the outer wall down into the old Jebusite City of David.

"You were very powerful today." Annias stroked his beard as they walked.

"God be praised," John replied softly, as he made his way down the treacherous stairway. "But nothing is achieved unless even the message is spoken in the name of love."

"I still struggle to understand all of these matters," Annias confessed, brushing past visitors who were ascending the dimly lit passageway.

"Truth and love," John instructed him, "must be the basis for all we do."

"Do truth and love ever collide? Can they conflict?"

Surprised by such a question, John slowed to consider what such a problem might mean. Clumsily John Mark bumped into them nearly knocking John off the step. "You never have done well in the dark!" John reached for the wall to keep from falling. Immediately, the boy darted on down the steps to avoid further censure.

"The dark?" Annias reached for the wall to steady himself. "Why did you say that?"

"He is always in the wrong place!" John laughed. "And his impetuousness and incessant curiosity will be the death of him yet! Perhaps you have heard what happened the night the Master was arrested? John Mark had been following us in the dark and was nearly taken."

"He eluded the soldiers?"

"One of the centurions grabbed him, but only got his cloak. John Mark broke loose, leaving the robe behind. He ran home naked!"

Annias laughed as they continued the difficult descent to the street level. When they reached the bottom and came out into the light again, John returned to Annias' question.

"Truth and love?" he pondered. "No one has ever asked that question before. Well, I think that genuine love will always lead us to the truth. Truth can be a hammer that breaks people into pieces, but true love heals and binds back together. Truth without love can be very painful and love that is not honest can be very destructive. Surely, there will be times when the truth would be a severe test of the validity of one's love. However, we must never be afraid to love! Love will redeem the truth."

"I find love to be more mysterious," Annias shrugged, "and much harder to pursue than truth."

"Ah," John smiled, "but truth is always to be tested and judged by love. And we have seen a picture of true love, for is it not the laying down of one's life for another?"

"Hum-m," Annias pondered, as he stroked his beard again. "Hum-m-m, I must think of these matters." Abruptly the tone in his voice changed, "It does occur to me that Thaddaeus blends both of the qualities together very well. He would do well in explaining such complex matters to Gentiles."

"You don't ever miss an opportunity!" John smiled knowingly.

"It's only an observation," and the diplomatic air slipped into Annias' manner.

"You no doubt want Thaddaeus to return with you to your country?"

"Ah, but is he not the perfect one? He is a solitary person who would travel well by himself."

"The apostles will be gathering this week and I am sure we will talk of sending an envoy to your land."

"And there is also a decision to be made about the shroud," Annias was cautious with his probing.

"Shroud!" John stopped in surprise. "You are still talking about that?"

"Is it not true," Annias raised his hand in a questioning gesture, "that a woman has come to believe because of it?"

"You must not let *your* love get in the way of the truth,"

John became firm. "Let us simply say a woman has come to believe."

"Yes," Annias persisted, "the woman called Alicia was added to our number as she contemplated the cloth."

"We are all trying to find our path through new ways. We still have much to learn, and must be patient. So many issues are still uncertain—but love will prevail!"

"Of course!" Annias quickly agreed.

The men nodded in mutual agreement and then turned to go their separate ways.

Across the city the shadows continued to signal that the business of the day was over. Although Thaddaeus' residence was often used as a place of instruction, no one had ever come there with the persistence that Alicia had shown during the past three weeks. The flighty casual inquirer had become recognized as a probing comprehensive thinker. Although it was unusual for a woman to come alone, the other apostles had noticed her natural leadership and did not protest her persistence. Each day she had appeared in the early afternoon with new questions and fresh enthusiasm. As she listened during the morning teaching times, her quick penetrating mind seized on the key issues, and wrestled with each implication of the apostles' doctrine.

During this afternoon Thaddaeus had also found her questions challenged his best thought. "So," he finished his instruction, "we are not trying to live by new rules. The old rules and laws have been filled with completely new meaning. We must express His way by how we deal with each other."

Alicia sat pensively, letting his words slowly enter her mind. She waited for him to say more.

"Love is the very essence of His teaching. To care for everyone we meet is the challenge He has given."

"But don't we care more about some people than we do about others?"

"Well, yes, perhaps," he replied, struggling to find the right way to better express himself, "but we are to treat everyone as though we loved them equally."

"I see—I think," Alicia answered, "but I still find it hard to believe that I can love everyone in the same way."

He dropped his eyes to the scroll before him, nervously shuffling it on the table. Clearing his throat, he seemingly couldn't find the right example.

"I can care for many people," Alicia explained sincerely, "but I wouldn't want to spend my life around them." Her words seemed instantly to drop a curtain between them. "Some of the teaching is hard for me to grasp," she said finally.

"Perhaps we have talked long enough today." Thaddaeus stood up abruptly. "I'm sure it is important that you not return home too late."

"Of course," Alicia said. "Few Jewish women come and go as I do. Simeon has always liked my independence. Ironically, he has now begun to worry about what I do with my time."

"He has noticed a change in you?" Thaddaeus continued to turn away.

"Of course," she said ruefully. "How could he not tell a difference?" She held out her plain, simple peasant robe and laughed.

"And does the contrast displease him too greatly?"

"I hope not."

Thaddaeus fumbled, "Our teachings should make you a better wife."

"They have made me a better person."

"I would hope you could be both," he said awkwardly.

Alicia caught an uncertainty in his reply and instantly her

face flushed. He had never mentioned Simeon before, and even saying his name felt like an impropriety.

"I understand," Alicia reassured him. She reached out and squeezed his hand. Then she was gone.

Not until long after Thaddaeus heard the gate close did he move. Once more, the room had become a place of shadows. He felt an almost irresistible urge to sink into the dusk settling around him, hoping it would rid him of what was lurking in the shadows of his memory. He felt perplexed and undone. Staring into the crackling fire on the hearth, he began to remember a day long past. . . .

The gentle lapping of the cold Mediterranean Sea was once again splashing his toes. He could hear the sea gulls as they circled the shore. In the distance, a girl, Alicia, was winding her way down through the rocky banks toward him.

She seemed to glide from one boulder to the other with the lightness of a gazelle. Behind her rose the distant walls of Caesarea.

Hidden amidst the rocks and caves of the barren shoreline of the coast, they could steal a few moments from the prying eyes of the villagers.

"You are just where you said you would be!" she laughed.

"And you came just as you promised!"

"If we're seen, you know the talk we will cause!"

"So," he pointed toward the large flat rock at the shore's edge, "let's sit down so that we'll be all the more difficult to see!"

She laughed and settled down to enjoy fully every second of their stolen time together. "What can an important man like the son of James want with a simple little girl from a poor family?" she giggled mischievously.

"Much," he said with a gentle warmth and ardor that made her blush.

Although he was ten years older, the difference in their ages was certainly not unusual. Jewish men customarily had an adequate income before contacting a girl's parents for her hand in marriage. However, Thaddaeus had directly pursued Alicia. Ignoring convention, he had talked to Alicia rather than to her parents. He had judged correctly that his family's prominence would allow him such forwardness. He had sensed her family wouldn't object to his impropriety. In turn, she had not avoided his eyes and advances, but had carefully and cleverly encouraged Thaddaeus in every way possible. However, she was not prepared for his boldness.

"I have watched you blossom like the lily of the valley in summertime," he said tenderly, "and I have seen you come forth as splendor in the spring. Now I understand the song that Solomon sang to his beloved."

Alicia fastened her eyes on the ground and said nothing. His every sentence fulfilled the desires of her heart and yet she was not ready for the overpowering effect of his words.

She knew that Thaddaeus could easily take control of men. She had watched at a distance as he directed business with amazing decisiveness. Now she realized he was taking command of her life with the same authority.

"I want to seal my future with you," he leaned closer to her, "and tie our destinies together. Do not ask me why, but I believe that the God of our fathers intends it to be so."

As her heart beat faster, her mind struggled to find the right words.

"I must have a sign from you that you know my words are true. Alicia, I believe you have the same message hidden in your love."

Her downcast eyes watched his hand spread out on the rock beside her own. His hands were not gnarled like a laborer's but graceful and artistic. Slowly she let her fingers slide along the rock until their fingertips were almost touching. There was a moment's pause, then she crossed the invisible line between them, declaring herself. Gently, but intentionally, she touched his fingers.

For an ecstatic moment, he knew what had passed between them. His hand slid into hers until their palms were tightly pressed together, their intertwined fingers sealing their pact.

When a smile slipped across Thaddaeus' face, they both began to laugh, like two children who had just broken every restraint of the adult world and had still escaped.

Thaddaeus reached out and gently traced the contour of her face, across her lips and down to her chin. Her eyes silently completed the terms of a commitment to a future together.

As the sun set on him that day, the sea and the silence performed their magic; the dreams of the past were fulfilled in those moments. Like sand going through an hourglass, the old was being poured out again with a new destiny and shape. . . .

The shadows of that afternoon by the sea faded into darkness in the apostle's room. Thaddaeus realized that dreams kindled by the seashore still smoldered in the ashes of yesterday. His yearning for Alicia had only been dormant in his heart.

The leaping dance of the flames before him confronted him with another memory. Simeon's explosive temper was like seering flame, and Thaddaeus had been burned by Simeon's wrath. His violent disposition for revenge had set the brothers against each other many times before Thaddaeus left home.

As he gazed into the fire, he realized yet another fearful truth. Should Simeon become angry enough with Alicia, his wrath would spare nothing.

In that moment, a new idea began to creep from the shadowy recesses of Thaddaeus' mind. What would Simeon say when he discovered his own brother had been his wife's teacher? A strange, diabolic sense of satisfaction grew as his thought expanded. At first he envisioned the shock on his brother's face in finding that his wife had become a follower of the Way. He could see Simeon's eyes widen in consternation when he learned that Thaddaeus had been instrumental in her change of heart.

Other images rushed to his mind. Always the opportunist, Simeon had enjoyed maneuvering Thaddaeus into situations which made him appear incompetent. Nor had Simeon wasted any time in consolidating his hold on the family wealth when Thaddaeus had left to follow Yeshua. Once more Thaddaeus felt the agony that had overwhelmed him when he heard for the first time that Simeon had taken Alicia for his wife.

Then the daydream took an abrupt turn! Alicia stood before her husband telling him that she still loved Thaddaeus. She chided Simeon with the towering superiority of his brother's virtue over his own arrogance. Thaddaeus could hear the young Alicia confessing her love for him. . . .

His dream dissolved as he recognized what he had tried to deny; he had never ceased loving Alicia. In all of the preceding weeks, he had not allowed himself to use the word or to confront what persisted in his heart. But now the truth could not be resisted any longer.

"O God, help me!" he confessed more than prayed. "I cannot deny what I feel. I love her and despise him!"

He shrank back from the fire as if to avoid any further revelation. In the ensuing darkness only confusion seemed to follow. How was it possible for an apostle to covet his brother's wife? Yet how could he continue to deny the truth?

That afternoon he had spoken confident words about love, only to discover that he hated his own brother. Now his words trapped and indicted him. Caught as he was between his convictions and desires, he found he no longer knew what was true or right.

Sometime in the night as the fire burned out, his head finally found rest on his arm and he drifted into sleep. When the rays of the dawn finally entered, they brought no greater illumination than he had known in the dark.

"Thaddaeus! Thaddaeus!" a voice sounded in his ears.

Struggling from sleep, all the apostle could see was a blurred form in front of him.

"Wake up!" the voice insisted. "It is already late in the morning!"

Slowly the face of John Mark came into focus, as Thaddaeus tried to understand what was happening.

"You must have been up very late," the boy said as he poured water into a bowl. "Unless you hurry, you will miss much of the meeting."

"Meeting?" Thaddaeus mumbled as he splashed water onto his face. "What meeting?"

"A special gathering was called for this morning to discuss taking the Gospel to the Gentiles. They are looking for you."

The words seemed to ebb and flow from Thaddaeus' consciousness like a receding tide. He found he couldn't quite grasp the meaning of John Mark's words.

"You and some of the leaders have been called together," the boy said, pulling Thaddaeus away from the table.

Slowly the apostle walked to the doorway and looked blankly into the courtyard.

"Hurry!" John Mark tugged at him. "You are already late and Annias insisted that I get you there as quickly as possible."

As they walked through the back streets toward the

upper room, John Mark kept up a running commentary of the events that were already unfolding.

"Simon had some strange vision that has changed his mind about everything," he chattered. "It happened to him while he was in Caesarea."

"Caesarea!" Thaddaeus nearly collided with a street vendor. "What was he doing there?"

"I don't know, but he was with important people."

"Who? What did he say about Caesarea?" Thaddaeus stopped, blocking the flow of traffic in the narrow street.

"That is why you're supposed to already be at the meeting! Don't stop now!" Refusing to answer his questions, John Mark pushed him on.

Turning the corner, they entered the unmarked passageway which concealed steps leading to their special room. Reluctantly, Thaddaeus followed the boy up the stairway. He was not surprised to see Annias outside, pacing back and forth.

"Where have you been?" Annias demanded, again becoming the royal dignitary of Edessa. "We are this very minute in the midst of the most important debate we have yet faced. There is no time for delay!"

"What happened at Caesarea?" Thaddaeus returned his impatience.

"Simon has changed his mind about the propriety of going beyond Israel," Annias tried to push Thaddaeus toward the room. "He had some dream or vision while staying at a Roman centurion's house. Now is the moment to urge the apostles to send one of you to Edessa!"

"Whom did he talk with in Caesarea?" Thaddaeus refused to move. Surely, he thought, Simon had heard about his family.

"If we go inside, we might find out," Annias answered sarcastically.

He knocked and the door opened quickly to allow entry.

The intensity of the discussion held everyone's attention on the figures in the center of the room. Thaddaeus was relieved that his arrival was unnoticed.

"I cannot explain how such things happen," the speaker was saying from the front. "I only know that the Lord has shown Simon a new truth from which we cannot retreat!"

Joseph surnamed Elias interrupted him. "I do not doubt his sincerity, but we are being asked to reverse convictions we have held from our childhood. We have always been a separate people!"

"No," an older man countered kindly. "What Simon has seen is not new. We have only been blind to what the Master was teaching us from the very beginning."

Even though Annias tried to move him to the front of the group, Thaddaeus sat down near the curtain. Sensing that a front seat might have some strategic value, the envoy moved on.

"You are asking us to believe that *our* Messiah has also come for the Gentiles," a perturbed young Jew addressed the older man. "Nicodemus, our whole history has taught us that we are to be a special people whom the Lord has set apart unto Himself. You ask us to forget the very laws that have preserved our purity and insured our identity."

"No, Joseph!" Nicodemus contradicted again. "Such ideas have only been expressions of our arrogance!" In a more conciliatory gesture, he reached out to pat the young man on the shoulder. "In many ways Yeshua tried to show us that we were only set apart to preserve a heritage that would make us more effective in sharing our blessings with the world. Did He not teach us to be lights set on a mountain? Did He not say that we were to be leaven in the loaf?"

The young man looked at the elder with bewilderment.

"He is right," John said, as he walked to the center of the room. "How often did we discuss among ourselves the irregularity of Yeshua healing those who were completely outside the House of Israel? It was then that He often chided us about their faith being greater than our own. Can we forget what He said to us when He healed the Syro-Phonecian woman? Her faith was commended as being greater than any found in Israel!"

Uproar filled the room as the men turned to one another in consternation. Some nodded agreement while others were upset and agitated.

The young man's voice raised above the confusion. "How do we know that God has revealed this to Simon? How can anyone know when Christ is truly being revealed to him?"

The elder smiled. "Joel, has God not always spoken to us in dreams?"

John added to the defense, "The Master has given us a key to understand these things. He taught us that the very essence of God is love. Whatever experience or sign causes us to have greater love is to be trusted."

John's answer brought Thaddaeus to his feet. "What do you mean?" he asked from the back of the room. "Explain more about what you are suggesting! We are to trust any experience that causes us to love?"

Shaking his head affirmatively, John addressed the group. "Simon's vision releases us from our old prejudices that kept us from loving the Gentiles. His experience forces us to recognize that Jesus meant for us to go into the whole world with His message. How can such an insight be anything but from Him?"

"Exactly!" another man exclaimed from the center of the group. "We were always called to teach the ways of the Lord to all the nations."

"Simon also said this Roman cohort in Caesarea knew your family," the elder abruptly said to Thaddaeus. "In fact, he learned many things from him that you have never shared with us."

Thaddaeus froze and he felt his face flush.

91

"The Roman holds your family in high regard. In fact, he knew that you left a great deal to follow the Master."

"Brethren," said John, moving forward to assert his leadership, "how can we deny what we are hearing? With signs and wonders God is confirming our call to go to the very ends of the earth. We have in our midst the leadership needed to teach us how to speak beyond the boundaries of Israel. Let us now in faith act on what has been given."

"Even more!" a voice interrupted John. "The opportunity is before you in this very moment." Annias stood up and turned to address the group. "Yeshua promised me to send one of you to Edessa to pray for our king. Now you have the confirmation that He wants you to fulfill His promise to me."

"Brothers, brothers!" the elder stopped him by raising his hands in the air. "We must not be swept away by our emotions. We must seek the Spirit's confirmation. Before any decisions are made, we must pray together carefully. Let us ask the Spirit of God to breathe on our thinking and bring us to such a singleness of mind so that we will know we are in harmony with the mind of Christ."

The suggestion silenced the group and without further debate each man knelt on the cold stone floor. Prayer shawls came up over each head, as one man after another extended his arms and turned his palms toward heaven. A faint murmuring of prayer filled the room.

The breeze began to blow through the window in an unusually audible way. As its sound and the prayers mingled, an unseen unity settled over the room. The force of the silent transaction left its mark on the soul of every man in the room—except one.

Thaddaeus could not pray. John's words had added to the unsolvable dilemma of the previous night. One phrase particularly confounded him. " . . . whatever causes us to have greater love is to be trusted." He could not dare to ask

John more about his meaning, nor could he fathom the nature of his implications. At the same time he wondered about what Simon had discovered in Caesarea. How much might he have learned about Simeon?

Confusion compounded confusion until finally, Thaddaeus abandoned any further pretense of praying and slipped behind the curtain. His usual sense of joy in being among the brothers had turned sour. Now he wanted to distance himself from them lest they learn too much. Quickly he was down the back steps and onto the street.

For the next hours Thaddaeus roamed Jerusalem, trying to sort through his emotions. He could not distinguish between what he wanted, what was right, and what he was called to do. The anonymity of the crowds in the market seemed to protect him. With his hood pulled over his head, he walked aimlessly among the vendors' stalls. Occasionally he would buy a fig, a handful of almonds, or some fruit. In the end he realized that he was simply waiting until the hour when Alicia would appear at his house; only then did he turn his steps homeward.

When the gate opened, he told his young servant, "This afternoon I want you to stay outside the wall. After the lady comes for her instruction, I do not want to be interrupted. We have a crucial issue to deal with today."

"Alone?" The servant wrinkled his brow. "Is this—" he stopped and nodded in compliance. Thaddaeus ignored the inference and went across the courtyard and sat down to wait.

By the time Alicia arrived, Thaddaeus' mind wasn't clear, but he felt a decision had been made. Though he had no sense of certainty, he thought that he knew what he was going to say.

"I'm here!" her happy voice called out as soon as the gate to the courtyard opened. The cloak and hood that still concealed her face were pulled back as she entered the house. "Am I late?"

"Whenever you come is the right time."

Alicia laughed and set a small basket on the table. "I brought you something I made to eat tonight. Let's say it is a small payment for my lessons. I have some difficult questions for you."

Thaddaeus sat down and motioned for her to sit at the opposite side of the table. "Where would you like to begin?"

"Last time you talked about the old laws made new and I have been thinking a lot about your meaning. You told me about caring, and I need to understand more about how we are to express such love. Perhaps we should start there."

Immediately Thaddaeus felt a loss for words. Usually, as soon as he began teaching, phrases and ideas seemed to leap into his mind. Now he was empty.

"Well?" she asked lightheartedly. "Do you have a better topic?"

"No," Thaddaeus replied very slowly, "that is exactly what I want to talk about, but I do not know how to begin." He stared into her eyes with such intensity that her entire mood changed and Alicia dropped her eyes to the table.

"From the time you left until late in the night, many things ran through my mind. I was forced to face what I have ignored for all of these weeks."

"I do not understand." She looked at the rough wood.

"I don't know how to say what I have come to understand! You think I have all of the right answers and now I know that I don't. Who am I to tell you what to do?"

"What has happened?" Her eyes slowly came up to his. "Something is different."

"What has happened is inside me and I do not have the words to explain it."

"This is not like you to be so upset. What has changed since yesterday?"

Thaddaeus placed the palms of his hands to his face and inhaled deeply. Rubbing his temples, he looked down at the table only to see her hand. Whatever had been his original resolution and intention, his deepest impulse obscured everything else. Slowly, he placed his large hand in front of hers, just as four years before, except that this time his fingers reached out for hers. The silence that followed was deafening.

"What—what is happening?" Alicia almost whispered.

Saying nothing, he began to caress her fingers. As the moment lengthened and she didn't move her hand, he felt he had his answer. Her face was flushed.

"I don't understand what path I have set us on," he sounded uncertain, "and I no longer know the way. I am only certain of one truth; I love you." His gaze deeply searched her face. "And I know you have never stopped loving me."

Tears began to fill her eyes and to slowly run down her cheeks. She bit her lip and clutched his hand.

"O Thaddaeus, when I first came to you, my intentions were all wrong! Then I would have tried to cause such a moment as this, but so much has changed. I have changed. I can't do anything that will harm you or what we believe."

"But you do love me," he persisted.

"I hated you at first. I really thought I hated you," and her tears came faster. "I tried to forget you when Simeon offered me the world—but I never did."

"And I never was able to really forget our pledge."

"Then I tried to bury my feelings after I found the Master," she added. "Truly, I tell you I have tried to erase any of those thoughts through my prayers, but I cannot if you give me any encouragement. I am not that strong."

Thaddaeus smiled. Her answers were more than he could have hoped to hear.

"You don't understand what you are doing," she warned

him. "Your world has been wrapped in a love that is pure. If we persist, you will find that this word *love* can have other connotations that come from my world."

"How can loving you be wrong?" Immediately he looked away. His own question accused him and he tied to dismiss the contradiction it begged.

"I am a woman, Thaddaeus. You don't realize what that means, but I do. There is no middle road in these matters."

"I would do nothing that is wrong," he insisted. "I just want to be able to love you. Perhaps we can be together," slowly he added, "in Him."

"Is that possible?" doubt rang in her voice. "Surely not."

"I don't know, but I want to find out," he sounded determined.

"Thaddaeus, I have already thought about us and I know one thing. I cannot love two men at the same time."

Even though Thaddaeus found satisfaction in her admission, he said nothing.

"If you encourage me, I will only withdraw from him."

"He doesn't believe anyway!" Immediately he felt the hollowness of such an answer.

"No, Thaddaeus, you have already taught me an idea that I cannot escape!" she shook her head. "Truth cannot be denied. We lie to ourselves only to our own detriment."

He reached out to her cheek. The touch of her skin filled him with the joy of her womanliness. His mind raced to find some justification for what he was doing. He felt caughtcaught between what he knew was right and the wonder of the moment.

"Is not any experience that causes us to have greater love," he struggled with the words, "to be trusted?"

CHAPTER SIX

Even though their eyes had adjusted to the darkness, each could only see the other's silhouette. After backing away from the window, Thaddaeus turned and embraced Alicia. Once more a whirl of emotion erased the questions he fought to ignore. It did not seem that two weeks had passed since they had crossed the line in their relationship. The last week was a blur as all barriers between them fell away. In that short time he had become as consumed with her as he knew she was with him.

"Do you think anyone will find us here?" Thaddaeus almost whispered. He had never seen this house before.

"We are perfectly safe," Alicia turned back the veil that covered her face.

He again looked out the window into the blackness of the night. "Still, it is very unusual for a woman to be out at night alone."

"My servant girl has no idea why I wanted to use her house, and Simeon won't return until tomorrow night. No one can find us here."

"You are warmth in the cold night," he said into her ear.

Silently her hands explored the contours of his strong back.

Although the darkness felt secure he sensed it robbed them of the fullness of their joy. "Shall I light a candle?" he asked with a smile.

"No, we must not give any indication that we are here."

Alicia pulled back the hood and removed her cloak. Before she could turn back to him, Thaddaeus moved behind her and pulled her against him. His hands against her small body could feel her roundness. He placed his lips against the back of her neck.

"These last days have been as a dream," she thought aloud. "They seem to have moved in minutes and yet to have covered a lifetime." After a long pause she added with uncertainty, "I'm not sure what is right or wrong anymore. I've quit thinking—I'm trusting you."

"When we are together, time stops while the hours race ahead." After a long pause he added with a sigh, "But the world doesn't wait for us to catch up."

"I don't want to think about such things tonight."

"But we must. My absence during the last days of debate has been noticed. There are those who wonder where I am. Already three of the apostles have asked if I am avoiding them; and they wonder why I am not taking part in the discussions."

"And I do worry that someone will realize that I am gone from home tonight." She turned to face him.

"Fortunately, Annias has decided I am trying to avoid being sent to the north with him."

"Sent north?" she gripped his arm hard. "Would they take you away from here?"

"It is possible."

"No!" Pain was in her voice. "That can't happen to us!" She pulled him even closer. "Don't let them!"

"Do you think I have come this far to let anything separate us again?" he assured her. "Long ago, I knew our destiny was set together." As the feel of her body became even more obvious to him, her closeness was its own intoxication.

"We must make every moment count," she held him tightly. "We cannot know what the future may yet hold."

"Then let us waste no time," he said, turning her around to face him. His hands reached through her hair as he pulled her face to his own and they were lost in their embrace.

Suddenly the door flew open and crashed against the wall. As torches lit the room, frightening shadows fell in every direction. Thaddaeus clutched Alicia tightly to himself to protect her. As the brightness of the light blinded their eyes, he could only make out the hooded forms of three men. He tried to shield his eyes from the glare that kept him from seeing their attackers.

"Look what we have here, esteemed elders of Israel!" a voice snarled from out of the dark.

"Simeon!" Thaddaeus and Alicia gasped at the same time.

"Well, my fine brother," each word was filled with sarcasm and hate, "you always thought I lacked your intelligence. But I had no idea you thought I was this stupid!"

"How did you find us?" Alicia's voice shook.

"Oh, now we have questions. Of course, your every word reveals your guilt." The flickering torches gave Simeon's hooded face a menacing, sinister shape.

"What do you want?" Thaddaeus tried to shield Alicia.

"My, my! Does it seem inappropriate that I might have come for my wife?" Simeon mimicked him. "Wanton that she is!"

"You followed me!" Alicia groaned in disbelief.

"Followed you? You fool, I have been following you for weeks! Did you not think that I would wonder at the strange behavior of such a cunning little creature?"

"Simeon, I can explain," Thaddaeus fumbled for some answer.

"Oh, can you?" he retorted tauntingly. "How fascinating for us to hear! At first, my wife begins retreating from all that my money buys. Next, she tries to become again the sweet, virginal village girl. Oh yes, I wondered what reason might lie behind these bizarre little reversals. Naturally, I guessed that it was all part of this new Messiah nonsense that has filled the city with madness!"

"And now it is time for us to purge our land of this new scourge of the devil!" one of the men snarled. "Let's start with him; he's one of their ringleaders!"

"What fascinates me most," Simeon ignored the suggestion, "is that our little flower of innocence is now ready to spread herself out like Bathsheba. Your new religion does do amazing things!"

"No!" Alicia protested. "It's not like that at all!"

"Do not blame her," Thaddaeus squeezed Alicia's hand tightly. "I am the one to blame."

"Your confession and concern are most touching to me," Simeon mocked cynically. "What I like most about your new religion is the unique way in which you play with the truth. You have these marvelous new laws which put you above the rest of us."

"Let's take them to the high priest right now!" a third voice demanded angrily. "Let's get it over with."

"However, Thaddaeus," Simeon pretended to instruct, "you will remember that our laws are still the custom of the land. Perhaps, somewhere in your memory, you will recall how we deal with adulterous women?" He had stepped into the light so that the glow gave his face an even more sinister appearance.

"You wouldn't dare!" Thaddaeus turned to pull Alicia away from the light.

"Let go of my wife!" Simeon's demand was slow and hate-filled. "Let go of her!" he suddenly screamed at the top of his lungs. Grabbing her wrist, Simeon pulled her across the room into the darkness behind him.

Immediately the other men moved toward Thaddaeus, thrusting their weapons at him. The dull thud of Alicia's body slamming into the wall carried above the shuffle.

"If you hurt her—" the sudden pain of a sharp point at his throat cut him off.

"You will what?" Simeon barely whispered. "Just what will you do?" he abruptly screamed. "Let me tell you what you will do!"

He paused and Thaddaeus knew that Simeon was fighting to regain his composure. Even in childhood, Simeon always had wanted to appear controlled and aloof.

"I always thought you were a little mad," he finally said condescendingly, "a little crazy, but benign. Now I find you have become a seducer of women, so I suppose we must take you more seriously. We must make sure that you do not trouble anyone else."

The sound of Alicia crying in the background added to Thaddaeus' agony, but he knew any movement toward her would jeopardize them both; utter helplessness gripped him and his mouth turned dry. He could feel the perspiration on his forehead as desperation clutched at his mind.

"You will leave Jerusalem immediately," Simeon's finger was only inches from Thaddaeus' face, "and if you don't, we will come to your meetings, to your leaders, and tell the truth about you! We will make sure everyone in Jerusalem knows what we have seen tonight. Before we are finished, we will have ruined the reputation of every one of your stinking followers of the Galilean!"

He brought his torch close to Thaddaeus' face as he stepped toward him. Then Simeon lifted the flame high so that its light illuminated both of their faces.

"The hour when you see my wife again will be the hour that seals her death. If you ever contact her, I will immediately drag her into the street. With my friends as my witnesses, I will cast the first stone and we will leave her dead beyond the gates."

"You wouldn't!" Thaddaeus begged in agony.

"Your arrogance is not above our laws!" Simeon said bitterly. "Alicia is my property, as are my cattle and my house. If she ever sees you again, I will not hesitate to finish tonight's business."

"I can't leave Jerusalem!" Thaddaeus protested.

"You will leave *now!* In fact, the only reason I hesitate to ruin you is that I don't want my name linked to yours." He lowered his torch until Thaddaeus felt its heat and knew the fire was dangerously close. "Perhaps you have also forgotten my capacity for vengeance? Let me leave you a little reminder, lest you doubt me."

In one quick sweep Simeon thrust his torch in Thaddaeus' face. The flames shot down the side of his face as the fire leaped at his hair and beard. Thaddaeus lurched backward, trying to cover his face with the thick sleeve of his robe. He heard the torch swish over his head and the singed smell of burnt hair filled his nostrils. A sudden hot pain on the right side of his face stunned him. In trying to avoid being hit again, he stumbled over a bench behind him and fell to the floor.

As he struggled to untangle himself, he heard the door slam. Groping in the darkness, Thaddaeus tried to get to his feet. The flash of the torch had momentarily blinded him and his eyes were still smarting form the heat. His heart was beating so hard that his breath came in gasps. Touching his face, he realized that a large portion of his beard had burned and shriveled from the fire. His right eyebrow felt like a stubble. Pain seared the side of his face.

Stumbling across the floor, he plunged out of the door

only to hear departing footsteps far off in the distance. He ran down the passageway between the houses to the street, but saw nothing; the sounds of departure were already lost in the maze of the irregular streets. Desperately he ran in the direction which seemed most likely. After turning only a few street corners, he knew any pursuit was futile. Yet he kept running.

What if he did catch them? The terms of the pursuit had been set for him! His hot, throbbing face was ample reminder that Simeon would fulfill his warning.

In desperation, Thaddaeus turned down another empty dark street. Twice he fell against sharp stones, bringing fresh blood to his injuries. His robe caught on a protruding splinter of a doorway, sending him to the pavement and ripping his sleeve. Only then did he allow himself to realize that running in the night through empty streets could only attract the attention of the soldiers. Without an explanation, he might find himself arrested.

Slumping against an empty doorway and panting in pain, he saw that he had no alternative but to return to his own quarters. Yet his mind raced from one idea to the next. Perhaps he could steal Alicia in the night. Or, they might flee the country. Once more he stumbled on a cobblestone and almost fell. Could he counter Simeon's rumors with his own explanation of his relationship with Alicia and still remain in Jerusalem? As he staggered on, he thought of the speech he could make to the apostles. But in the end, one dilemma could not be solved. There was no way to escape the penalty of the law of Moses and the vengeance of Simeon's temper. And there were witnesses too. By the time he reached his house, despair had engulfed him.

Since his entryway had long since been bolted for the night, Thaddaeus was forced to pound on his own door and to shout an explanation to the young servant boy.

"Do not disturb me!" he pushed the confused boy aside.

"I must be left alone!"

"Your face!" the boy cried as the moon's glow lit up the courtyard. "And your hair! What has happened?"

"Let me be!" Thaddaeus cut him short. "Do not allow anyone to come near."

"But you need help—" the boy reached out. Thaddaeus left him standing by the door as he disappeared into the house. Dumbfounded, the boy stared at the closed door.

Engulfed by darkness, Thaddaeus slumped wearily down on the bench and let his head fall into his hands. Waves of hopelessness washed over him.

Only then did he realize how long it had been since he had truly prayed. He must pray, he thought, but how? He was both drawn and repelled by the words of the petition he tried to make. At every level he felt abandoned.

"O God, help me! I don't know which way to turn. Help me; please help me!" His fist banged down on the table. There was no breeze to stir the curtains and the night seemed stifling. He felt perspiration running down his back.

"Please don't abandon me in this hour of my need," he pleaded. "What am I going to do? What will become of us?" The room was a void in which his every emotion taunted him. The hollow echo of his voice mocked him and even his sobs seemed to laugh at him.

"I need You!" he cried. "This is the hour of my greatest need!" He began to pound on the table again and again.

"Are you all right?" a voice timidly asked from the porch.

Now the fear of what the servant might have heard gripped him. Though he realized how loud he must have been, he answered angrily, "I told you not to disturb me. Leave me alone!"

All he could calculate was his loss. Alicia was gone. The future was stripped of hope. His world had become a desert of emptiness.

Searching for some answer, any answer, his mind seized

on a strange thought. Was it not in this very room where Alicia had made her discovery? While he had discounted the value of the shroud, any source of strength would be better than his present abyss of emptiness. Slowly he made his way to the chest and lifted the lid, took hold of the bundle and made his way back to the table. In his despair Thaddaeus abandoned all reservations about handling a burial cloth, and ran his hands over the linen. Then he grasped it tightly and began to pray:

"Be here! Be here with me! I must know You haven't left me. You promised You would give me a Way that the world could not take away!"

The emptiness mocked him—he was only talking to a piece of cloth. Then, anger pushed other emotions aside.

"No! No!" he screamed into the night. Lifting the cloth into the air, he hurled it toward the chest in the corner. He no longer knew what he believed about anything. Hopeless and despondent, he fell into his bed. Darkness became his cover until weariness sealed shut the night.

The next afternoon three apostles stood with Annias behind the curtain which opened into the upper room, sharing their hopes for the new decision that had been made.

"Have you seen Thaddaeus?" Annias asked.

"No." Simon looked away and seemed troubled.

"I am concerned about him," John said thoughtfully. "I told him that he seems to avoid our fellowship. He spends too much time alone."

"I trust he will be here for the discussion." Annias nervously wrung his hands. "We are coming to the critical moment."

"Some of the believers are having a very difficult time accepting the idea," Bartholomew observed.

"Yes," John agreed, "but these are the same people who

struggle most with the meaning of love."

"In time, truth bears witness to itself," Simon added confidently. "Even now, most have come to see from the Scriptures that Israel's mission always was to reach and serve the world."

"I know that many of the believers are prepared to take the message to the four corners of the world," Bartholomew assured the group. "A new day is truly about to begin!"

"I marvel," Annias pondered, "that such a consensus has been reached and also at the harmony that followed your debates. Once the group began to pray, differences seemed to end."

"Well," John said thoughtfully, "truth and love should always blend together in perfect harmony."

"Absolutely!" Simon agreed. "In the mind of God, there is perfect harmony. When we are reflecting His mind, we dwell together in unity, even when our opinions differ."

"Already Simon sounds like a Greek philosopher!" Bartholomew jested. "The world cannot wait to see this fisherman turned teacher."

The group laughed as they parted the curtain and entered the gathering. Annias made his way toward the front and Simon called the group to prayer. After the silence and the final Amens, Simon began, "My brothers, truly I perceive that God shows no partiality. To Israel, He sent first the good news of the peace that comes by Yeshua the Christ. Then we saw the proclamation extend beyond Galilee and out from Judea. Now we know that God has granted new life to the Gentiles. The time has come to discuss our mission to the larger world."

"I wish to speak," a young man held up his arm.

"What would you say to us, Barnabas?"

"Many of our people have been scattered because of the persecution that arose when Stephen was stoned. I have friends who now live in Phoenicia and Cyprus. My own relatives have fled to Antioch. All that these people need is to receive word of our decision and they will begin work among their neighbors. In fact, many have already begun preaching in these cities."

"In what way?" Simon asked.

"My sister tells me that in Antioch, the Greeks now call us Christi-an-ios, people who belong to the Christ."

"Christi-an-ios?" Simon contemplated the meaning.

"Perhaps we should begin by sending messengers wherever our people have settled," Barnabas concluded.

A murmur of approval went around the room.

"In that instance," another elder observed, "none of the apostles would have to leave Jerusalem. We could keep our council here and Jerusalem would always remain the center of the church."

Once again the group indicated their approval. Annias, however, stood to object.

"My friends," he quickly interrupted, "I think we must not overlook the importance of having the apostles' special wisdom to guide new churches which will start in the Gentile world. Even greater maturity and guidance will be required in the strange lands beyond."

The group was momentarily confounded by his suggestion. He searched their faces to see if his argument was being received.

"Moreover, Yeshua Himself told me that an apostle would be sent to Osrhoene, my country." He waited for his blunt assertion to have its full effect before he continued. "Therefore, let me humbly suggest that we choose one of you to accompany me beyond the mountains."

"Wait, wait!" protested James, the son of Alphaeus. "We are moving much too fast. Careful consideration must be given to each detail."

Discussion broke out in groups around the room. As Simon attempted to bring the discussion back to an orderly flow, Annias searched the room to find Thaddaeus. He quickly made his way to John Mark.

"Where in the world is he?" Irritation blazed in his eyes.

Intuitively knowing who he meant, John Mark shrugged his shoulders.

"Find him quickly and I will double this," Annias said, pressing a gold coin into the boy's hand. Then he stepped back to the center.

Another half hour of discussion was required to bring the debate back to the point where Annias had left it. Once the group agreed that some apostles should be sent out, they moved on to other decisions.

"I want to make a most prayerful request," Annias once again stood up. "Thaddaeus has already been attested to as having gifts for working with the Gentiles. I believe God has already ordained that he return with me to the north."

"Certainly the two of you have become good friends and are quite compatible," John observed.

"Thaddaeus has not been a part of our discussions as of late," James looked about the room. "Might that convey a reservation on his part?"

"Perhaps he has anticipated such a call and is leaving all things in God's hands." The diplomat hoped his wide-eyed look of attempted innocence was not obvious.

"I have felt it would be good for Thaddaeus to be away from Jerusalem for awhile," the inflection in Simon's voice clearly implied more than he stated.

Once again, nods of approval moved through the group indicating unanimity of opinion.

"Brethren," James, the brother of John began, "it is with hesitancy that I speak, but I feel a great urgency about these matters. Perhaps I should not speak thus, but I am troubled by a dream I have dreamt twice."

"Have not dreams always served us well?" Peter smiled. "Do not be reticent."

"I must conclude that the Lord is speaking," James said heavily. "Twice I dreamt that a great sword was sweeping through our midst and we scattered in many directions to avoid the blade. Then, it turned and came for me. Just before the sword fell on my head, I heard the words from above, 'Well done, good and faithful servant.' Then the dream ended."

Silence fell over the room. None seemed to want to comment.

"We continue to hear rumors," Matthew added, "that King Herod awaits the right moment to strike. Perhaps James' dream is meant to warn us."

"I do believe," James added, "that we must make all haste in sending out our ambassadors. Even tonight, we should set apart Thaddaeus or Barnabas or any others that feel called to go."

Ignoring the ominous tone of James' message, Annias felt only joy. He envisioned himself on the road home. At that moment, Thaddaeus entered with John Mark. The sound of the door shutting caused the group to turn.

"Good heavens!" Peter pointed. "What has happened?"

The group was stunned by Thaddaeus' appearance. He had tried to pull part of his hair back to the right side, but a large gap of missing hair was obvious. Large chunks of his beard were gone and his cheek and eye were fiery red. His limp sleeve clearly revealed the tear.

"See!" James pointed. "Even now the attack has begun!"

"No, no," Thaddaeus motioned them away. "I was attacked, but I am all right." Quickly retreating from their attention, he sought his usual place near the curtain in the back. "Please," he insisted, "the damage is only slight. I will be fine in time."

"Perhaps this is not the best time to talk with you," Peter began again, "but what we have been discussing involves your future. We want to make sure that you agree."

Thaddaeus looked apprehensively at Peter.

"We believe that the Lord would set you apart to leave with Annias and to share the Gospel of peace in his country. We have discussed the matter and feel assigning you the task is right. Would you accept such a commission?"

Thaddaeus' mind went blank. Slowly, he extended his hands as if he was trying to form some reply out of the air. Finally his arm dropped as if in acquiescence.

"Wonderful!" Annias exploded. "Nothing stands in our way to leave at once."

"Tonight, as we partake of the Body and Blood, we will set you apart for the Lord's special use." Simon smiled as if many things were settled.

"One more matter does beg your attention," Annias hung onto his moment of opportunity. "I would ask your blessing in taking the shroud with us. It will be of great use in our country."

"There is a limit to what we can change," Simon stiffened. "The objects of death are still contaminated!"

"Do not forget what has happened in your midst," Annias argued. "A woman's life has been changed. The shroud was part of the metamorphosis."

"Yet we cannot ignore the fact that the image is still of our Lord's uncovered body," another apostle interjected. "Such a display is not seemly."

"Please, please!" Annias raised his hand to ward off the debate. "I have heard all of your concerns during the past weeks and I have an answer to each problem. Let me show you my solution."

Walking to the wall, he picked up a square package. Pulling back its cloth cover, he exhibited a silver encased picture frame. The frame appeared to be about eighteen inches square and three inches thick and the back was sealed with a flat piece of wood.

"The shroud can be folded so that only the face will be

seen," he explained. "The rest of the material will remain folded and hidden in the back of the frame. A small door will protect the material."

"Hm-m, ingenious." John held the frame for a moment and then handed it to Simon.

"You are very clever," Simon turned the metal shape over, "but I still can't understand why you have such a conviction about this shroud."

"I am sure you can appreciate the large expense required to construct such a silver frame of this size." Annias pushed ahead as if to settle the argument.

"There is another problem here," Simon looked blankly out the window. "The law forbids us to make any graven image or to worship any representation of God. Could this shroud become such a representation?"

"Even from my childhood, I have been warned about violating this commandment," Annias answered, "so I do not take the matter lightly. Yet in Osrhoene there are other representations which I believe would not violate the second commandment. They are called *sooras* or, as the Greeks say, icons."

"I have never heard of such a thing." Simon started to lay the frame down.

"An icon is a picture that depicts spiritual and inner reality. Of course, it would be not only wrong but impossible to ever make any actual picture of God." Annias gestured enthusiastically to seem totally emphatic in his orthodoxy. "But icons are doorways to the spiritual world. In the same way, any drawing of the Master could never fully depict the truth about who He is, but would help one see beyond the flesh." After a pause he added, "Human hands did not construct the picture on this cloth. That fact cannot be ignored."

"Surely we all agree with what you are saying," John interrupted, "but how is an icon any different from a graven image?"

"Ah!" Annias smiled. "An icon is the opposite of an idol. An idol is for worship, but an icon shows the spiritual truth that leads one on to worship the true and holy One, blessed be His Name. It depicts the eternal and helps us find the realm of the divine. I believe that the image burned into this linen is the true icon for the Gentile world."

"I have never heard of such a thing." Simon shook his head. "What you are describing is foreign to us."

"Yes," John agreed, picking up the frame again, "but we are dealing with mysteries that exceed everything we have known in the past. We must be open to all of the new things God is doing as we move into the strange world outside of our country." Thoughtfully, he turned the frame over studying it carefully.

"Perhaps," Annias argued, "this linen is visible Scripture. Maybe what we are seeing exceeds the power of words to describe."

"I can appreciate our problem in knowing what to do with this linen." Thomas arose to speak. "I feel the same reluctance about it," and his voice trailed off for a moment, "but I also know the power of touching and seeing. While our Lord commended faith which does not require evidence, He did not condemn those who need assistance." He glanced around the room and several heads nodded affirmatively. "Who knows what the future may yet hold for this relic of the resurrection? I say that we send the linen with them!" His voice was authoritative and final.

Simon pondered his words for a moment, then shook his head. "Perhaps, Thomas best understands such matters," he sighed.

After a long silence, the matter appeared to be settled. As Annias sat down, deep satisfaction was evident on his face. His mind was racing ahead, planning the many details of returning to his homeland.

After the final prayer, the diplomat turned to find the apostle standing behind him. "God's will has prevailed!" Annias extended his hand. "We have opened a new door to the world!"

Thaddaeus only stared at him with a sullen look that fell like a pall over Annias' enthusiasm.

"You are hurt?" Annias' eyes darted back and forth from the seared beard to the torn robe.

"Do you always win?" The apostle's face was blank and his voice was flat.

"Surely these issues are larger than someone winning or losing. They are beyond personal considerations."

"I'm sorry," the apostle's eyes were cold and hard, "but tonight the sky will be very dark. In the morning we will leave this place and I will never return again."

"Never return? Come now! I see no need to be so morbid!"

"You are going home, and I am going into exile. It is that simple."

"Please," Annias pleaded, "Edessa is a long way from here, but it is not in another world."

"Another world?" Suddenly Thaddaeus took command of the conversation. "What do you know of other worlds? I once told you that when Yeshua touches a life, one world ends and another begins. Perhaps even I didn't understand what I was saying, but I tell you that He does make worlds to begin and end. Before we are done, maybe even you will learn about how worlds can abruptly come to an end!"

Leaving Annias stunned and silenced, Thaddaeus walked out the door that opened across the rooftops. Once again, the sun was setting and night would soon fall. He studied the roofline and the contour of the city wall, trying to etch each detail in his mind.

"The sun sets," he said to himself, "day dies, and my world ends."

CHAPTER SEVEN

The bitter cold of the mountain night wind cut through even the heaviest cloak. "Do you speak Syriac?" Annias asked, throwing another stick on the fire.

"Not well," Thaddaeus replied quickly, "but I know enough to converse. Syriac is very much like Aramaic."

"Well, most of our people speak Greek also, so you should have no trouble being understood."

Annias had particularly enjoyed speaking Hebrew in Jerusalem. He seldom had opportunity to use his family's language outside of their home in Osrhoene. Yet, as they traveled the desert highways north, he and Thaddaeus had increasingly conversed in Greek. Slowly but completely the little world of the Jews had vanished before the vast expanse of the Graeco-Roman Empire that was truly the world.

"Our people are the proud remnant of the great Hittite Empire. They were a civilized people even before Alexander and the Greeks marched on us. You must respect their heritage," Annias cautioned.

Thaddaeus only nodded and continued looking into the

fire. The dance of the flames seemed to have completely captured his attention. Both men huddled close to the heat. Although the rugged, arid terrain appeared like a desert by day, at night the high altitude brought biting cold.

"Though you have said little about yourself over these past six weeks," Annias ventured, "you have certainly been a good traveling companion."

Thaddaeus merely nodded. Looking down at his dirty cloak, he realized how they must appear, in their soiled, patched traveling robes. They had dressed like beggars, to lessen the threat of being robbed in unguarded passes and on treacherous trails.

"I know how difficult it was for you to leave Jerusalem," Annias probed further.

"I can say the journey has been fascinating," Thaddaeus changed the subject. "Even the torturous passage from Damascus through the desert to Palmyra was not without its meaning."

"The desert can burn many things out of a man's soul," Annias observed philosophically.

Thaddaeus answered only with a grim stare.

"At any rate, tomorrow we will enter Edessa and our journey will be ended!" Annias slapped him on the back.

"My journey has only begun," Thaddaeus corrected him. "These past weeks have clarified for me what being an apostle means. I suspect that I am destined always to be a sojourner."

"Who can understand such things?" the diplomat replied sympathetically. "Is it not possible that Edessa could become your home? Why could not our city be the center for a work that would extend to all the Syriac peoples?"

Thaddaeus pulled his cloak more tightly around his neck. Such a suggestion seemed to chill him more.

"There are a number of things we must discuss before tomorrow," and Annias' tone became professional. "We will enter the city without notice or fanfare. I want to keep you in seclusion until well after my return is announced. We must handle these procedures very carefully."

"Why?"

"These are times of intrigue. I do not know what has transpired during my long absence. Perhaps there are those who will not welcome my return."

The wind suddenly swirled through their little camp and sent sparks flying up into the night. The embers lasted only for a moment before an opaque blackness closed in around them.

"What are you suggesting?" Thaddaeus narrowed his eyes.

"The night is overtaking us. Let us sleep that we may arise with the sun and begin our journey before the day is upon us."

Thaddaeus reflected on other times he had seen Annias spin his own little webs of intrigue. Along the way Annias had left small hints that the state of Osrhoene could well be in political turmoil. Yet, Thaddaeus had discovered that he no longer cared about such things.

As days of travel had blended into weeks, a plodding, routine dullness had infected Thaddaeus' spirit. He did only what he was supposed to do, and had little awareness of spiritual reality. The closer they came to the borders of Osrhoene, the more anxious he was about his ability to fulfill Annias' expectations. He sensed the darkness of the desert night was not unlike the darkness he felt within his soul.

Barely had his eyes closed, it seemed, when he was awakened by Annias. Thaddaeus' sleep had been fitful, and he awoke with a tiredness that reached his bones.

"Let us say our prayers before the first rays of the day break across the hills," Annias urged, as he moved about the camp in a nervous, quick manner.

Even in the gray dawn they could see the rolling mountains which surrounded them on all sides. Tall thin cedars and pines dotted the mountainsides and blended into the scrubby shrubs and thistle of the dry desert ravines. The arid air made their faces leathery and their lips parched.

Pulling their prayer shawls over their heads, both men entoned the "Shema, O Israel," and then each silently petitioned for his personal needs. Annias finished first and soon had his horse packed and was ready to ride.

"Come on, come on!" he chided Thaddaeus. "You are the slowest man in the morning I have ever seen! We still have ten miles to ride before we enter the gates!"

Without reply, the apostle slowly gathered his gear and mounted his horse. As they turned north and crossed the final pass, they saw Edessa on the high plateau before them.

The horses picked their way down the rugged terrain, past huge boulders. Thaddaeus reflected that traveling in these mountains and ravines was not unlike the journey from Jerusalem to the Dead Sea. The rock-strewn lands could surely support only a few goats and sheep. As they wound their way past the huge rock outcroppings, he was amazed at the sight of strange figures cut into a boulder.

"I see that the great goddess Arinna has caught your eye," Annias observed, drawing his horse up short. "Look to your left and you can see Kamrusepa, the god of medicine."

"What are these carvings?"

"They are the ancient gods of the Hittites in whom most of our people still believe. For 1,300 years, this religion has ruled the land."

"Your people pray to these rocks?"

"If it were not for the failure of Kamrusepa, we would not be here today. When prayers to him did not avail, I was commissioned to go on my long journey. You should thank him as we pass by." Annias laughed, moving them forward again.

They finished their descent and rode out onto the flat plain that led straight toward Edessa. A large riverbed with dry sandbanks reminded them that in this land water was life.

"Our people believe the gods determine the course of all events," Annias explained. "Many claim that the gods make their will known through dreams and oracles. Affairs of state may be determined by a vision."

"Do you believe that these pagans have received the truth?" Thaddaeus asked.

"Perhaps not," Annias smiled, "and then again, there may be more reality in such dreams and visions than we know."

"Come now!" Thaddaeus scoffed at him.

"Who knows where our dreams reach? Perhaps they tap some stream that flows beneath all of life. Does not even Jehovah send His messengers along that flowing current?"

Ahead, other travelers appeared and moved parallel to them as they continued toward the great city. Annias kept urging the horses on. The more he tried to increase their pace, the more reluctant Thaddaeus seemed to be. The old diplomat continued his running historical discourse as if he were briefing a government courier.

"While the victory of the Greeks made us part of the Seleucid Empire, we always maintained an independent spirit. For 160 years we have been a free government. We have the autonomous Cappadocians and Armenians to the north. None of us have succumbed to the Romans." The galloping of their horses finally made conversation impossible and further lessons of history were lost in the dust.

The walls of the city rose on the horizon. The number of travelers increased as caravans of camels and donkeys merged together before the huge gates of the city. As the edges of the plain met the walls, numerous flat-roofed stone houses appeared. Herds of sheep and goats mingled among the converging flow of travelers. Everywhere the fine desert dust rose in the air, only to fall again on the visitors coming and going to the city.

As they reached the edge of the city and passed through an enormous ravine, Thaddaeus noticed that the city walls seemed to be only partially completed. Workmen were still extending the height, and the ancient entryway looked in need of serious repair.

"Edessa is, indeed, an ancient city," Thaddaeus observed, as the horses slowly climbed out of the ravine.

"There is no record of our beginning. Perhaps the city has been here for 2,000 years."

Blending into the crowd, they pushed their way through the great bottleneck of the ancient stone gateway. Annias' eyes sparkled and snapped, and Thaddaeus sensed his jubilation that the journey of many weeks was coming to its end.

Once inside the walls, the whole city opened before them. In front of them was an enormous plaza which extended several hundred feet in every direction. While the herds of animals and the caravans of travelers moved through the center of the open space, vendors on each side of the gate called out news of promising marvelous bargains. Everywhere Thaddaeus looked he saw people who were strangely different from himself. The fabrics and patterns of their robes, their headdresses and turbans were different from anything seen in Israel. The men wore baggy trousers, and the women elaborately decorated tunics. Although the people had the same olive skin, the shapes of their eyes and faces were distinct. Now he knew why Annias had never been completely accepted as one of the Edessians.

119

"Annias! Annias!" rang out across the square, over the confusion and rumble of the market. At once he was off of his horse and pushing his way through the crowd. Losing sight of him, Thaddaeus dismounted and began looking at his new world. The wares piled against the base of the city walls caught his attention first.

A woman in a bright dress sat in front of piles of skins and bundles of wool. With her strangely shaped spindle, she was carding the fluff into yarn.

Turning away, he noticed that a woman whose dark brown robe covered her head and body was staring at him from beneath her hood. Her cold black eyes were so deeply set that her furrowed brow gave a sinister appearance. Thaddaeus smiled and nodded, but she only stared. He felt very much like the stranger he was.

His eye caught the piles of water jugs that lay behind the wool merchant's bin. As he looked at the fascinating shapes, the thousand smells of the market filled his nostrils. The strange blending of herbs, noontime heat, animals, and people made him feel slightly nauseated.

"A-a-a-h!" someone screamed from behind him. Thaddaeus whirled to see a large man falling forward, a spear sticking in his chest. Before he knew what was happening, cries sounded from the wall at the opposite end of the market.

"Death to the enemies of the King! Death to those who oppose Abgar! Kill the Ras El Khuden!"

Horsemen charged into the crowd and swords flashed in the air. From walkways along the wall, other warriors leaped into the crowd. Instantly, the courtyard turned into an arena of terror.

"Kill the traitors! Murder the renegades! Kill Ras El Khuden! Butcher them!" was heard in every direction.

To his horror, Thaddaeus saw both old men and children being trampled in the push of the crowd. Frantic people ran in every direction, seeking refuge.

"Kill them! Let their blood serve the king!" rang in his ears. Suddenly, two men pushed him backward and in the next second, a boy who had run toward Thaddaeus abruptly froze; his eyes widened and his mouth dropped open in a silent gasp of pain. As the boy dropped to his knees, Thaddaeus saw the point of a metal blade protruding through the left side of his robe. With a savage jerk, a soldier pulled back his sword and the youth fell dead on the stone pavement.

The soldier charged forward like a wolf cornering his prey. Terrified, Thaddaeus stepped backward, only to fall into piles of clay jars. As he tumbled into the vessels, they avalanched on top of him. The hollow sound of breaking clay echoed in his ears as a large pot crashed against his head. His heart beat wildly—at any moment, the sword might run him through.

When he was able to find his feet and stand up, he was confronted with an even more amazing sight. Three feet from him, a soldier was laying on his face. The back of his neck had been so deeply hacked open that he was nearly decapitated. Thaddaeus' whole body convulsed and the blood pulsated in his temples. Everywhere he looked people were dying, and their cries filled the marketplace.

At that moment a huge man leaped from the wall and landed on top of Thaddaeus. His size and great strength allowed him to easily overpower the apostle. With his powerful arms locked around Thaddaeus' neck, he dragged the apostle along the wall and prevented him from regaining his balance. An enormous hand reached around and covered his mouth.

Somewhere along the wall a door opened and Thaddaeus was hurled into the darkness. The thick wooden door shut and a timber dropped down to secure it. When he tried to stand up, his attacker yelled in Syriac, "Stay down! Do not make a sound!"

The door sealed out the light but not the sounds. The battle raged for what seemed an eternity, as cries of murder and terror rang out. Only when the confusion slowly subsided did Thaddaeus remember that Annias was on the other side of the square when the attack began. He would have been standing where the first men were killed. He could only suspect that the worst had befallen his friend.

He became aware of a stench of rotting hay, and decided that he was inside a storage shed built into the great wall of the city. But all that Thaddaeus could see was the shape of his abductor peering through a crack in the door.

"They are retreating," the man said to Thaddaeus. "The end will come quickly."

He could hear the sound of horses riding out through the gate; the screams subsided and the square grew quiet.

"Now!" a voice yelled from the other side of the door. "Leave quickly!"

When the door was pushed open, a small old man in a multicolored turban gestured frantically for him to go. Before Thaddaeus could decide on his course of action, his huge abductor yanked him up by the cloak and pulled him through the entrance. Everywhere he looked he saw a scene of horror—men and women were strewn across the square, many obviously dead and others hideously wounded. Blood-splattered cloaks lay around the bodies. Debris from the merchants' stalls was everywhere. Moaning and crying had replaced the battle cries. Thaddaeus frantically looked for some sign of Annias, but all he recognized was his own horse lying on the stones, its belly slashed open.

"Move!" the old man with the turban demanded. "We have no time to waste!"

As the three raced along the wall, Thaddaeus found himself nearly being dragged. They charged down a side street that led out of the large square. Stumbling past the flat-roofed houses and stuccoed walls, they disappeared into the inner city.

After ten minutes of running through the alleys and back streets of Edessa, Thaddaeus was pulled inside of a high wall and another gateway of large timbers shut behind him.

Panting and breathless, the three men slumped to the floor of a large courtyard. In the center, a magnificent fountain was splashing cold water. Thaddaeus looked up at an enormous mansion and saw servants running to assist them. The chatter of Syriac was so profuse that the apostle could understand nothing of what was said.

"We are safe," the old man assured them, removing his turban. "Let us go inside."

"We have survived," the large man grunted.

"Where am I?" Thaddaeus asked in bewilderment.

"You will know in time," the old man assured him. "First, come into the house."

"What is happening?" The apostle's eyes darted back and forth across the courtyard.

"Do not worry," the large man assured him. "You are among friends," and his voice sounded cordial for the first time.

Having no recourse, Thaddaeus followed them into the mansion. Everywhere he looked, statues and rich tapestries told him that he was in a house of a very wealthy man.

"Please sit down," and the old man placed his turban on the table and let his outer robe fall away. 'I know you must be very warm after such a chase. The servants will bring us refreshment."

"Please tell me where I am and what has happened!" the apostle implored him.

"You are in the house of Annias. Fortunately, you have survived a battle between the princes of Osrhoene. If the two of us had not been at the gate, you would probably have been killed."

"They are maniacs in their drive to take the crown." The large man scowled as he stood towering over them like a bodyguard.

"But what of Annias?" the apostle broke in. "What has become of him? I fear for his life!"

"No more than I do," the elderly man assured him. "He is my brother."

"Your brother!" the apostle gasped.

"Indeed," he nodded his head gravely, "I am his older brother. However, do not despair, for long ago I learned that he has a special skill for surviving. I can only hope his wits have served him well today."

The servants interrupted him as they brought in cups and a large jug of wine.

"Let me formally introduce myself. I am Omri," he began again. "Annias and I have served the House of Abgar for many years. My companion is Egon the Armenian, who has been our protector and trusted friend for many years."

The large man bowed politely to the apostle.

"I am Thaddaeus." He bowed in response.

"We know," Omri answered. "We have been expecting you. When you were in Damascus, Annias dispatched a message about you and your arrival. We have been awaiting you for a number of days. We honor you as the answer to the problem which plagues our land."

Once again, both men lowered their heads as if to salute a superior.

Thaddaeus felt unsure of what to say. "I am only a simple man. . . ."

Both men smiled and nodded as if to acknowledge his humility. His apparent modesty seemed to increase their esteem for him, but their reverence only increased the uneasiness he felt.

"Now we must send men into the city to discover the fate of my brother." The old man motioned to the bodyguard and Egon left immediately. "Allow my servant to give you a room that you may rest while I join the search."

As Egon left, a servant ushered Thaddaeus to another part of the house and up a flight of stairs to a room overlooking the courtyard and beyond to the whole city. Even Annias' residence had been chosen for its strategic location.

Beneath him, Thaddaeus saw a rambling city of flat-roofed, mud brick houses, blending together in a brown blur which ran down meandering streets. Centuries of stopping and starting again had given Edessa its irregular shape. As he looked out to the very edges of the city, he realized that Edessa was not walled at all. Travelers entered a citadel with extended walls, but long ago the enormous city had outgrown the protecting confines of the fortress.

Everywhere Thaddaeus looked, Edessa was calm and life appeared to be routine. Only then did he recognize the strange inconsistency of the fierce battle at the gate and the tranquility of the rest of the city. Everything about the situation baffled him. Annias had given hints of conflict, but no warning of an impending war. Each question only led to another. Who were the soldiers trying to kill? Moreover, who was the Ras El Khuden the attackers sought to assassinate?

Strange faces, dying faces, new faces, her face, all floated before his eyes. As the afternoon passed, the intense heat of the plain rose up and his reflections were muddled and confused. Drowsiness overtook him and the many faces blended together into a dream of killing and terror.

Shadows were falling when shouts of the servants awoke Thaddaeus. People were running through the courtyard beneath his balcony, and the air was filled with excitement.

"They are here! Come quickly!" rang from below. "They have returned!"

Rushing to the window, Thaddaeus could see Egon, the giant Armenian, closing the outer door to the courtyard. Suspecting the worst, he rushed downstairs and into the large gathering room which was already filled with people.

"Annias!" Although his dirty travel robes were stained and torn, the dignified envoy held his gray head erect with a bearing that signaled that any injuries were to his dignity only. "You survived!"

"Of course!" Annias said smugly. "They will have to do much better to kill the Ras El Khuden."

"The Ras El Khuden?" Thaddaeus asked. "Who is that?"

"I am! That is my title as the chief servant of the king!" His voice betrayed irritation at such a question being asked in front of his own servants.

"They were trying to kill *you!*" Thaddaeus exclaimed in dismay.

"Sit down." Annias gestured toward his couch. "I have much to tell you. The attempt on my life was meaningless. It only expressed confusion. Osrhoene is in a great turmoil and we must act immediately. There are many serious problems before us."

"Abgar is not far from death." Omri sat down on a large cushion. "The princes fight over who will take the throne. Today you were caught in such a battle. It seems someone has already learned of Annias' return."

"If Abgar dies," Egon folded his massive arms across his chest, "the entire province will be plunged into war!"

"You must understand," Omri continued, "that the king's survival is crucial. Because of his illness, Abgar is unable to stop this feuding. Even the attack you survived was stupid and pointless."

"How did you survive?" Thaddaeus turned toward Annias.

126

"It is even as David said of him who dwells in the shelter of the Most High: 'A thousand may fall at your side, ten thousand at your right hand, but it will not come near you,' " he stretched to stand even a bit taller.

"Thank God we have lost nothing this day," Thaddaeus sighed.

"We have lost a great deal!" Annias said abruptly. "When my horse was finally found, the baggage had been stripped. The frame with the shroud has vanished!"

"Stolen!" Egon's arm swished through the air like a sword.

"Even now the search goes on," Omri reassured them, "but I suspect we will not find these objects easily. Even if a beggar or thief stole from your horses, he will be hunted. The princes know that the return of Ras El Khuden means that a cure has been found. They too will search for all of your possessions."

"Our hope," Annias removed his dirty outer robe and motioned for the servants to take it away, "is that for a period of time they may think I was wounded or killed today, and that no one will understand the value of the shroud."

"You must remember," and Thaddaeus' gaze went from person to person before returning to Annias, "that I place no great value in this linen. Perhaps losing it is gain."

"No!" Annias stuck his finger close to Thaddaeus' face. "You are wrong. He turned to the group in a manner that asserted authority. "I have not told you of the story of the shroud. Now is the time for you to know!"

He motioned for the servants to leave while gesturing for Egon and Omri to sit down. "I have already told Omri and Egon something of the history of the shroud so that they would understand the urgency of my search. Now you must know the whole story."

Egon shut the doors to assure their privacy. The dimness

of the late afternoon shadows seemed to further insure them of the seclusion of their conversation.

"Something deep within me stirred the first time I saw the shroud. I knew this strange burial cloth would be a special instrument of God." As he talked, Thaddaeus looked down at the floor. "I knew it had a part in my mission on behalf of the king, but those were only premonitions. Then I heard Alicia tell her story. Only then did I open your chest and truly study the linen at great length."

"And," Thaddaeus cynically interrupted him, "what happened?"

"Nothing. At least nothing happened that afternoon. I returned the bundle and left unnoticed, but that night I began to dream strange things. In fact, night after night, the image on the cloth burned in my sleep. Finally, I realized that there was a pattern to all of these dreams."

"Is not my brother like Joseph in Egypt?" Omri pulled at Thaddaeus' robe, but he did not respond. "He is revered among all of the counselors of the king because he has always been able to dream marvelous things. My brother has a very deep spirituality."

"What sort of pattern emerged?" Egon's deep thunderous voice sounded childlike.

"At the end of each dream I would see the king gazing on the face of Christ. Even as he looked, the color returned to his face and strength came back to his arms. My dreams have made me believe that the shroud is a crucial part of the cure of Abgar."

Instantly Omri and Egon barraged Annias with questions. What did the face look like? What did he mean? How could such happen? However, the apostle only leaned back in silent contemplation as an unexpected sense of relief fell over his mind. For the first time in weeks he saw an answer to a dilemma in which he felt trapped. Annias had now given him an excuse for the failure that he felt certain was ahead of him.

Thaddaeus recalled how for seemingly endless days he had felt empty. His prayers were only words formed from rote memory. The flow of swift moving events had carried him along, the tides and winds of circumstances moving him as they pleased.

As they had crossed the desert, again and again he had searched through his experiences with the Master, trying to remember how He touched the sick and instructed the apostles to do the same. Yet, Thaddaeus knew there was no power in his hands.

Months before, during the Feast of Pentecost, a glow of power had filled him wherever he went. He saw the reality of God everywhere. He would awaken in the mornings to joy and go to sleep at night with peace. But now he was alone in a desert.

Into this drought an answer had come. The disappearance of the shroud gave Thaddaeus the excuse he needed. Annias' despair was his consolation.

"Perhaps we are doomed to failure," Thaddaeus said quietly.

"No, no, no!" echoed around the room.

"Never!" Annias roared. "The Almighty did not take Israel out of bondage for no reason, and He did not lead me across the desert for nought!"

"My brother," Omri said, "I do not understand all that you have told us about the new Messiah, but I have never doubted your wisdom. Never have I questioned how God has put His hand on your life through these many years. I believe you will know what we must do."

"Remember how the psalmist has instructed us," Annias told them solemnly. "God promised, 'I will protect him, because he knows My name. When he calls to Me, I will answer him; I will be with him in trouble; I will rescue him and honor him.' He will yet be with us."

"What shall we do?" Omri turned to Thaddaeus. "Annias tells us you have special gifts granted by this Messiah."

Thaddaeus was silent until the moment became awkward.

"Now it is time to call on His name," Annias finally instructed them. "From our childhood we have only known the names of Adoni, of El Shaddai, and of Elohim. Now we have a new name, that of the Messiah."

"What is this name?" Omri asked urgently.

"Yes!" Egon urged. "Tell me that I may also call on Him."

Quietly, but confidently, Annias, the pupil, began to teach. As the apostle listened, he realized that the ever-deepening shadows had completely covered him. The brother and the Armenian strained forward, yet he leaned back aback and lowered his eyes.

"For I deliver to you as of first importance what I also received," Annias continued, unfolding the story. Thaddaeus' mind drifted back to Jerusalem.

CHAPTER EIGHT

For more than a week, Annias made no demands on Thaddaeus. No matter what the subject, the apostle declined again and again to make comment or offer any opinion when questions were asked. He left in the morning and returned late at night, always giving the same excuse: he was searching for the stolen shroud.

Whatever Omri and the servants thought, they also refrained from asking questions and allowed Thaddaeus to do as he pleased. He had become a strange, solitary figure moving mysteriously about the fortresslike house.

Meanwhile, Annias was able to keep his reappearance in Edessa bathed in mystery and had not yet declared himself to the king. Informants said that the attack on the citadel was only a skirmish between two of the princes and that his title had been invoked simply as part of the confusion of the moment. However, all felt that Annias' life could well be in danger.

During the long evenings, members of Annias' household and a small group of confidants gathered around the fire in the huge hall to hear the old diplomat talk of all that he had learned in Jerusalem. Often going late into the night, the discussions appeared to Thaddaeus to be intense, when night after night he returned late and slipped past the doorway, going silently to his room.

After days of walking the streets, the city became monotonous to him. One street seemed to be no different from another, and Edessa offered little to hold his attention. Thaddaeus' freedom was his bondage. His reclusive existence caused time to hang heavily upon him.

After two weeks, the more colorful main streets and thoroughfares of Edessa were boringly familiar. The only thing left to see was the terrain beyond the boundaries of the city. He had noticed that the city appeared to stop at the foot of a particularly jagged mountain which rose abruptly out of the plateau.

"Perhaps," he thought, "if I climb the slopes, the distant plains might reveal something new and different. I must keep moving!" It was as if some unnamed fear would catch up with him if he stayed too long in any one place. An inner gnawing chewed on him if he sat still.

Here and there, groups of women stood huddled together sharing the morning gossip. With their heavy scarves pulled across their heads and then doubled back to conceal their faces, only their black eyes peered out. When they stared briefly at Thaddaeus, their concealment made each of them seem an enemy or spy. Traveling on, he watched women weaving on large wooden looms. Occasionally a team of oxen lumbered by, pulling huge carts which rolled on giant wooden wheels. The scenery was predictable.

At the end of the city stood strangely eroded boulders that were menacing in size. At the final bend of the city street, a dust-covered old blind man sat on the ground with his back propped against one of the large rocks.

"Alms, alms!" he called, with his head cocked as he

listened for the slightest sound. He held his hand extended with the palm open. "Alms, alms, for those who have need!" he repeated with a steady consistent rhythm. To his dismay, there was nothing in his coin pouch.

"Alms, alms for those who have need!" The beggar's eyelids were open, and scars across the lenses of his eyes made them white. His disfigured face was repulsive.

Hearing Thaddaeus pause, the beggar further extended his hand upward. "Alms, alms, for those who have need!"

After Thaddaeus walked away, the realization of disappointed expectation set in and the beggar began a new chant. "Blind are those who have eyes but will not see!" He waited a moment, then his chant became a taunt. "Blind are those who have eyes but will not see!"

The incline of the road became more abrupt. Clearly Thaddaeus could gain a better altitude by climbing straight up the bank. Yet, the beggar's accusing face would not leave him, and the words kept ringing like a personal interrogation: "Blind are those who have eyes but will not see."

Climbing quickly, Thaddaeus paused to look back over his shoulder. The sparce shrubbery was so much like the mountainsides in the wilderness of Judea. "Prophets and holy men live in the desolation of such eroded heights," he thought. "These places strip one of the influence of the world. They clear the mind." He stopped again to catch his breath.

On and on he went, moving among the rocks. Trying to keep from slipping, he wiped the perspiration from his brow. As the sun rose in the sky, the temperature climbed quickly. Already he could see the whole city sprawled beneath him, and for the first time he comprehended the pattern that made the many parts a whole.

Although the blind beggar had become only a dot, his words climbed up the mountain: "Blind are those who have eyes but will not see!" Shrugging his shoulders, Thaddaeus clambered on toward the summit.

Most of the rocks were sharp and jagged, but some looked like well-rounded loaves of bread. Only then did Thaddaeus also realize that he had not made provision for anything to eat or drink, and dryness clutched at his throat.

"What's the matter with me?" he said aloud in disgust. "I don't even take care about myself anymore, but walk around like a man in a trance. . . as a blind man."

Pushing on, he edged his way between boulders and crawled up through the huge cracks in the megaliths. Even though he thought about stumbling onto a spring, he knew finding water was completely impossible amidst such barrenness. Near the top of the mountain he spotted what looked like a shelter under a pile of the broken and eroded boulders. To his delight, he saw that a cave had formed underneath the rock overhang. The cool cavern would offer escape from the increasing heat.

He had been searching for just such a vantage point. In all directions he could see clearly completely out to the horizon line. To the west was the mountain range he had crossed entering the plain that led to Edessa. Beyond those peaks lay the world of the Romans. Far out to the south stretched the desert lands that caravans crossed to travel to Egypt. Beyond the east horizon were the mysterious places about which he knew nothing, except that traders brought rich silks from those lands. In a strange way, he felt he was able to survey the kingdoms of the world from his little cave. The cavern felt like a hidden place in his mind where he could find thoughts that he had long since concealed from himself.

"Had I not become an apostle, I would have been a rich man!" he said emphatically to himself.

A small desert whirlwind swirled up the side of the mountain, carrying dirt in every direction. Thaddaeus pulled his cloak about his face to shield his nose and eyes.

As the wind subsided, he looked out again onto the desert kingdom at his feet. From this height it appeared lifeless, flat, and strangely empty. "My life has become a wilderness," he mused.

Time passed slowly as the lonely man stared at the scene beneath him. The vacant eyes of the blind man kept appearing before his own clouded vision, and his words came to Thaddaeus' mind again and again. The strange contrast of sitting on top of the world and possibly being blind at the same time poked at his thoughts. He allowed his mind to drift as memory seemed to follow memory. Childhood experiences floated across his mind.

The sun moved beyond the high point and started its journey toward the west. Thaddaeus kept resisting the paradox, not seeing what he had experienced which demanded that he remember. Even the heat conspired, turning his unfaced questions into burning irritating issues. He thought of Alicia and Simeon. And as he remembered being alone with her, he tried to escape the accusation of his own conscience. Somewhere in the middle of the afternoon, he gave up the struggle and allowed whatever had been bottled up inside of him to be released.

At first the thoughts came in a trickle, and then he was buried by an avalanche of hidden memories that had been ignored, random pieces of a puzzle suddenly fitted together with startling precision. He found himself confronted by painful realizations that accused rather than acquitted. As soon as one issue had been dealt with, another would immediately arise and begin its own round of interrogation. As the afternoon drained away, his awareness of time returned. Though racked with pain, he felt his life finding the synchronization with the world that it had lost during the previous months.

Near the end of the afternoon as the impact of his thoughts overwhelmed him, Thaddaeus lowered his head into his hands and began to weep. As the tears streaked his face and beard, they turned into little streams of mud. When his hands wiped his eyes, dirty paths were left around them. Finally, it seemed that all of the bitterness that had been inside of him was gone, swept away as if by a great flood. He felt exhausted and at the same time exhilarated. With a deep inner sense of confirmation, he rose, and cried to the winds, "It is finished." Slowly he began his descent down the barren mountain slope.

His pace increased with each step until he was almost running when he reached the bottom. The beggar was gone, but Thaddaeus paused a moment before the stone where he had been, and then moved quickly on through the streets toward Annias' house.

As soon as he entered the house, he asked a servant to bring the writing material and ink to his room. After dousing his face with cold water and taking some refreshment, he began to write.

"I must remember everything," he said to himself. "I must not let anything be lost." He unrolled the blank scroll of parchment the servant had left and lifted the pen.

"O reader," he began in Greek. He paused and was surprised that he had not chosen Hebrew to reveal his innermost thoughts. Something at a very great depth had truly changed within him.

In this moment I open my heart to you. Perhaps on another day there will be those who question my integrity and authority as an apostle. Possibly they will be correct, for surely I am not worthy of what has been given me. Nevertheless, in this moment I can write only of the truth that I have discovered. Personally, I know that I can no longer judge anyone.

While climbing the mountain, I descended into the caverns of my own mind. Standing on the heights of the peak and peering into the recesses of my soul, I now know what I have refused to acknowledge. Truly, none are as blind as those who have eyes but do not see.

I have found the secret room hidden in my soul. Long ago, the Master told me of this place. He told me that in this chamber live dreams of power and wealth, the lure of security and prestige, the enticement of pleasure and lust. Only there can a person know the fullness of temptation. Today I have looked into my own soul and seen the truth.

When the Master bade me follow, it was with the promise of what I could become. He offered me forgiveness for my hollowness and taintedness. While I followed gladly, other intentions remained hidden at the core of my very being. Cleverly and deceptively I kept these truths even from myself.

In the beginning when I knew I had found the Messiah, I expected Him to depose the Romans and establish the throne of David in Jerusalem for all eternity. I thought a special place would surely be reserved for me. With such prominence, I would exceed the accomplishments of any of my family. Truly, the threads of deception were woven into my cloak of righteousness. Although the resurrection vastly changed my expectations, pretentious ambition still lurked in the shadows. My sin is not so much that I have violated the commandments as that my motives are corrupted by pride.

He put down his pen and painfully remembered how, even in childhood, he hated having his superiority challenged. He realized that his loathing of Simeon had really begun when the importance he sought did not manifest itself as political power in the Messiah's kingdom. His resentment had grown out of frustrated self-interest.

As he thought of Alicia, the pain was nearly overwhelming. When he considered what must have become of her, he wept again. Thaddaeus knew that his deceit had corrupted all it touched. So recently, his selfishness had eroded the promise in their relationship.

"My love was void of the truth or I would not have jeopardized her life and her newfound faith," he thought. "I rejoiced in the wrong and that has cost her dearly." He started to write again when another thought struck him. "I love her yet." The pain was lodged in his soul. Finally he wrote:

So now, even my loneliness is but a result of the vanity that resides within me. The deceptiveness of pride is without limit.

While I am unworthy of the mantle placed on my shoulders, yet will I pray as did David, "Create in me a clean heart, O God, and put a new and right spirit within me. Restore to me the joy of Thy salvation!"

This day I prostrate myself before His promises. I truly give Him my future. I seek no more than a small and insignificant place to serve. I must never judge or measure truth by any man's representation of it. O reader, seek truth for its own sake. Should you find value in me, lay this to His credit. Let the rest be a warning about the corruption that lurks within the flesh.

I do not seek to rule any realm save the one that resides within. Though this be my confession, my witness is that blind eyes can yet be made to see.

Thaddaeus bar James

As he affixed his name, the light of day had almost vanished. While he felt hunger from missing two meals, he did not think he could eat, and so he turned and stretched out across the couch. Closing his eyes, he was overwhelmed by his own fatigue. For the first time in months, he slipped into a deep and restful sleep.

Thaddaeus didn't stir when Annias entered his room an hour later. Holding his candle high to illumine the whole room, the old man quickly noticed the scroll spread out on the table. Annias shielded the light with his hand so as not to disturb the sleeping apostle, and began reading the scroll carefully. With each line his eyes widened. He stared at the extraordinary document for a long time, then blew out his candle. Placing a cover over his friend, he paused to pray and then left the room so that silence could do its work.

Thaddaeus slept so deeply that he hardly moved during the night. From within a strangely vivid dream, a distant voice began beckoning him. "Get up! Get up and come out," seemed to echo from another far-off mountaintop.

"I'm asleep," something inside of him said, "and yet I'm awake. I am floating in a twilight world of my own inner realities."

Once more the voice demanded his attention, "Get up and come out!"

"Who's calling me?" he tried to open his eyes but couldn't. "I know that voice—and yet it cannot be!" The brisk morning air made him want to pull the warmth of his covering closer. "No, no, it cannot be His voice. Surely it is not His bidding! And the night air is so cold! Do You really mean for me to arise?"

"Get up!" abruptly reverberated through his mind with relentless authority. "Come out from among them, for I would speak to you. Be separate from those memories, for I have given you a new day."

Although his eyes were closed, his mind was alert enough that the absurdity of his responses was clear to him. "Why am I longing for sleep and warmth when the Master is calling me? Why do I linger? Maybe it is a dream that will vanish in a moment."

Only then did he begin to see the light, a glow that

originated more from within than without; and a voice came from the center of the light. Without having to open his eyes, a radiance penetrated everything around and within him. Once more the command was given, "Get up and come out from the past, for I would speak with you!"

Thaddaeus turned back his cover and stood up. The cold of the stone floor shocked him. Yet, still the glow and the voice persisted with increasing power and magnitude.

"You asked once how I would reveal Myself to you and not the world." The peace-filled voice sent joy pulsating through Thaddaeus' very being. "You have forgotten My answer."

"My God and my Master!" Thaddaeus gasped aloud, dropping to his knees. "I am not worthy!"

"My Word is the Word of the Father and he who loves Me keeps that Word." Each syllable penetrated to the center of Thaddaeus' mind and body. "I live where that Word is obeyed."

"O my Lord!" Thaddaeus cried out, feeling he could not stand the magnitude of the spiritual ecstacy that was engulfing him. "I cannot bear it."

"I live where there is a contrite heart and a humble spirit. I abide with those who tremble at My Word."

"Depart from me," Thaddaeus sobbed. "Depart from me, for I am unclean. I am no longer worthy to be numbered among Your followers."

"In your brokenness you will be made whole," the voice moved even closer. "Only the unworthy become worthy."

"Forgive me!" Thaddaeus covered his face. "I cannot be what You have given me the gift to become. I cannot represent You before the world!" As he spoke, he looked fully into the brilliant light and perceived a pure white mantle being extended to him.

"This day I claim you again! I do not ask you to go *for* Me; I call you to go *with* Me. Listen for My voice before you speak; seek My mind before you decide; wait for My direction before you act. The way is prepared unto eternity."

The radiant white mantle lowered upon his shoulders. Instantly he fell prostrate on the floor, as if overpowering Omnipotence would consume him. In that second, he was ready to die and to be swallowed by the glory.

"Look only to Me!"

Then the vision began to fade, but the words still burned in his mind as if imprinted by a branding iron. Lost in what he could not yet comprehend, Thaddaeus knew that at last, he was completely understood.

His lips formed silent words of praise over and over again until his own words were lost in utterances that seemed to come from the inner recesses of his soul.

He had no idea how long he lay on the floor, lost in prayer and praise. The light and the voice had long since ceased, yet the fullness of the experience burned in him so powerfully that he knew he could not be in the presence of another human being just now.

Leaning against his sleeping couch, he drifted into another prayer, lifting all that was within him up into a glorious unity with the very essence of the Spirit of God.

"What has happened?" he murmured aloud, as he considered the nature of his experience. He could not decide whether the encounter had been within him or from the outside. "Would others have heard the voice and seen the light?" he asked. Whatever the verdict, the lingering warmth and joy was ample evidence to him that he had not imagined what had happened.

After sufficient time had transpired that he felt he could again enter the world of humanity, Thaddaeus called a servant to prepare a bath and to bring fresh clothes more suitable for Osrhoene than his own.

When the servant laid out a heavy, dark blue robe with gold threads woven into panels, the apostle instructed,

"Please tell Annias that I wish to speak with him." The man nodded as he laid a gold-braided waistband beside the robe and new baggy trousers. "If he is here, ask him to meet me at the gathering room as soon as I am dressed." The servant bowed and left the room.

After bathing, Thaddaeus groomed himself, sensing that each action was further completion of a new person. As he donned the robe and gold belt, the metamorphosis seemed complete. He felt ready to appear publicly. A modest calmness made him aware of a new gentleness in his spirit. Slipping from his room, he set out to find his host.

Annias was standing before a long table, studying several scrolls which were unrolled before him. Stroking his gray beard, he was pondering what he read.

"My friend," Thaddaeus addressed him.

"Good heavens!" Annias looked up in surprise. The transformation astonished him. "You are looking well today!"

"I have much that I must say to you," and the apostle moved quickly to the table. "I must confess to you several truths which I have kept hidden."

Annias gestured toward two chairs facing each other and sat down.

"For the last few months I have been a poor example of what I have professed to believe. I have much for which to ask your forgiveness."

Annias held up his hand as if to halt the confession, and shook his head implying that further explanation was unnecessary.

"No," Thaddaeus continued, leaning on the table. "I must face the truth in your presence. There are many things you do not know."

"All that you have already said is quite sufficient."

"Perhaps when you understand the whole matter, you will think differently," Thaddaeus insisted. "Even as late as yesterday, I was considering leaving and going away to some other place. I was ready to lay aside my calling as an apostle and to lose myself in a strange land where I could start over again.

"Occasionally we all have such feelings." Annias gestured once more as if to dismiss further conversation.

"You do not realize the magnitude of my errors." Thaddaeus looked down at the table. "I still wonder if I can be of any value."

"You do not need to tell me anything. I accept you just as you are."

"But you do not know!" the apostle protested. "While we were in Jerusalem, I found I loved Alicia. I have not only loved another man's spouse, but I have also coveted my own brother's wife!"

"I already know all of these things," Annias quietly looked away.

"What?" Thaddaeus bolted forward.

"From the first time I mentioned her name to you, I knew something existed between you. I watched your eyes when you talked and I saw the hidden embers of love becoming a fire again. Yes, I knew what was happening."

"But you never said—" Thaddaeus dropped into the chair. "You gave no hint."

"I knew that if the Master chose you, He saw in you the strength to deal with such a temptation. I perceived a goodness in you that would not allow evil to triumph."

"All of these months you have known!" Thaddaeus' words faded and his eyes filled with tears. "And you have still trusted me?"

"I have never doubted you."

"Oh, but I doubted myself! And worse, I allowed bitterness and resentment to be at home within me. I let despair blind me to all who were around me." After a few moments of silence he added, "I even jeopardized the fellowship of the believers in Jerusalem."

"We understood your struggle, but felt you would have to face it alone."

"We? What do you mean by 'we'?"

"Simon and I discussed the matter at length when he returned from the house of Cornelius in Caesarea. He learned the whole story of Alicia there. Simon knew that I had introduced her into the fellowship, so he sought me out. We talked and convenanted together to pray daily for your well-being. I have done this every day."

Thaddaeus put his hand to his lips and shook his head in amazement.

"We agreed that I should leave quickly for Edessa in order to alleviate your struggle. When you returned with your face burned and your robe torn, we asked no questions but feared the worst."

"It was the worst," Thaddaeus lowered his head into his hands.

"Now we must forget what is behind us and look to what God has ordained for this land. We have work to do here."

"But I have failed with your brother and friends. I have even hidden in the marketplace from all of you."

"Now I will make my confession," the old man patted him on the hand. "I know what you have been doing and all of the places you have gone. You have been followed every moment you were out of this house."

Thaddaeus just looked at Annias, no longer having any capacity to be surprised.

"I could not let you face the dangers of this city alone. The political instability is too great for you to be unprotected. So now you have something to forgive me for."

"You are the most incredible man I have ever met! You can even manage to make a confession of error sound like an opportunity."

Annias smiled and stroked his beard.

"I have one more thing to say," and Thaddaeus stood up. "I have fled from any form of ministry. I had nothing left to give you or your family—much less to your king. But out of the crucible of my pain, the Master has chosen to recast my life. He has again placed His Spirit within me."

"Praise God!" Annias exclaimed, lifting his arms in the air. "I have been praying for this moment."

"Now I must wait on what *He* chooses to give me. I cannot go on my own. That is over."

"Wonderful! Wonderful! This is, indeed, God's doing!"

"I am trying to tell you that I do not have the confidence in myself that I once had!"

"Marvelous! That is God! You have no choice but to trust Him!"

"Please, Annias, you must realize my limitations!"

"Hallelujah!" the old man almost danced. "Even now, Omri, Egon, and the others are gathering for the noon meal. You must speak to them this very moment!"

"No, I'm not sure I'm ready yet," the apostle said falteringly.

"But God is!" Annias thundered as he gripped Thaddaeus' arm and pulled him toward the door. "This is the day God has made!"

Annias charged on through the door with Thaddaeus in tow, guiding him down the hall to the dining room. The others were seated, but they stood when the two men entered.

"The apostle of the Lord is truly among us now!" Annias almost shouted. "This man who has been especially chosen by the Lord is ready to speak to us. Let us hear him gladly."

As the group of eleven applauded, Thaddaeus recognized two faces he had noticed on several occasions in the market and realized that they had been part of his protection. "Forgive me," the apostle began. "To shun the fellowship of brothers is a grave error. Once before I did not seek the

145

counsel of the believers and I erred greatly. I will do much better in the days before us."

Omri stood and bowed to him. "My brother has been sharing with us all that he learned in Jerusalem. He tells us that it is possible for us to know the reality of the Messiah, but such thought is beyond our grasp. Would you help us understand how this can be?"

Thaddaeus lowered his eyes for a moment and silently breathed a prayer. "Obedience to His Word," was instantly on his lips. "When we follow His teaching with fidelity and integrity, He becomes known to us."

"Oh! Ah!" Murmurs of insight went around the room and Annias nodded agreement.

"But how can we begin such a journey with Him?" Egon asked.

"You must ask His Spirit to enter your life, and seek to hear His voice speaking in your heart." Thaddaeus moved to the head of the table. "Even as you breathe in the air, you must ask His Holy Spirit to invade the inner world of all you think and feel and want."

"Show us how to do this!" one of the men urged him.

"It is like eating food," Thaddaeus slowly looked down on the table. He studied the meal spread there and then picked up one of the pieces of thick flat bread and a wine goblet. "Receiving His Spirit is much like taking food into your body." Extending the cup and the bread toward them, he was surprised by the authority in his voice. "Let me explain how. Yeshua said He would always be with us. On the night that He was betrayed, Yeshua took the bread and gave it to them saying, 'This is My body. . . . Take, eat.' "

CHAPTER NINE

"Our little group has grown in size and depth since you began to teach," Annias said, as he presented a friend to Thaddaeus, after an evening teaching time. "This is my friend, Addai." A small man in bright blue attire stepped forward.

Annias continued, "The word is spreading rapidly throughout the palace that someone very special has come to Edessa. Soon the king will hear your message."

"We will be praying for that moment," Addai said, as he extended his hand to Thaddaeus.

"It is my pleasure to know you," and Thaddaeus gripped his hand.

"Addai is a maker of silk goods and special headdresses," Annias explained. "He makes the magnificent gold headdresses of the king."

"I can only put something on people's heads, but you put wonderful things in their minds." Addai pumped his hand.

"And together we will change their lives!" Thaddaeus answered, as he waved good-bye.

The apostle watched as the last of the group departed,

feeling a deep sense of satisfaction with how the evening had progressed. Something special had been added to his words, and the final prayers had been deeply moving. At the same time, he was humbled by his acceptance in the gathering.

When the last person was gone, Annias turned to Thaddaeus. "The time is almost ripe for you to see the king. I know you are ready now."

"I will have to pray much tonight, I must not just *go* to the king—I must know that I am sent."

"Surely, surely," and the older man sat down. "Of course, we have one more matter that must be settled before the moment is fulfilled. The shroud must be found."

"Please," Thaddaeus said sitting opposite him. "There is no use in discussing the cloth. By now it has likely been destroyed."

"No, I cannot deny my dreams. Always they have been crucial in how God guides me. I know that you must not see the king until the shroud returns."

"Truth is truth," the apostle shook his head. "God needs no evidence to accomplish what He alone can do in a human heart. If the Spirit is to touch the king, it will be by God's choosing; there will be no need for a special sign."

"You are a great teacher who understands many things of which I know nothing, Thaddaeus. Yet, I may know something of matters that have eluded your experience. I cannot convince you, I know, but I believe that the shroud is a part of what God intends to do among the people of Osrhoene."

"The Spirit opens our eyes to the need in our hearts. The inner witness of truth is what changes people. Pictures and signs may only muddy the water."

"No," Annias held up his hand. "There is no contradiction between what I have seen in my dream and what you are saying. It is all a matter of how God chooses to use what He has given."

"I'm sorry," and Thaddaeus stood up, "but I would not be interested in the shroud even if it were here!"

"Well," Annias smiled, "it may still come to that. The king has asked to see you and I have delayed the matter twice."

"You have already talked with him?" Thaddaeus' eyes widened.

"I waited as long as I could to make my presence known. Then I very slowly gave him the details of your return with me."

"I appreciate your keeping me so well informed!" Thaddaeus started for the door.

"You must remember that the ways of diplomacy are often circuitous and clandestine."

"So I have observed," the apostle said rather dryly over his shoulder.

"I only have been trying to balance many delicate aspects of this whole matter," the envoy protested. "You must appreciate the subterranean war for the throne that is being waged by the princes."

"I leave such matters with you," Thaddaeus' voice trailed off down the hall.

Early the next afternoon, the apostle was walking through the garden when the servant summoned him. "Come quickly, O gracious one," he called to the apostle. "My master calls you on urgent business."

Immediately Thaddaeus followed him into a small office that Annias used for personal business. Much to his surprise, a strikingly beautiful young woman in rich dress was in the room with the diplomat.

"Come in, come in," Annias gestured. "A most extraordinary thing has happened."

The look of aloofness in her large black eyes was obvious

and she carried herself with an air of condescension.

"You are in the presence of Magyar," Annias slightly genuflected, "the wife of Hannan, son of Abgar, Prince of Osrhoene."

"I am honored." Thaddaeus bowed in the gesture that acknowledged royalty.

"She has come to me with a very interesting concern and has brought us a most unique gift."

"We are humbled by your interest." The apostle knew well how to make the appropriate response.

"Magyar has also heard of the teacher from the south who is a disciple of the Great Healer of Israel, and she hoped to give him what she has found." Annias nodded to the princess and she snapped her fingers twice.

A servant girl entered through the opposite door carrying a cloth-wrapped package which she extended to her mistress. Without a word, the princess untied a leather thong and held up her present.

"The shroud!" Thaddaeus gasped.

The silver frame was scratched and the corner of the glass was broken. Nevertheless, the ochre-colored image of the face was just as it had been the day the linen was packed for the trip from Jerusalem.

"Where did you get this?" Thaddaeus picked up the frame.

"Allow Magyar to tell you her whole story. You will be amazed." The princess looked at the door and the servant left, shutting the door behind her.

"Your highness, this is the apostle of whom you have heard," Annias pointed to his friend. "This is Thaddaeus."

"If it please you, O great teacher, I will tell you not only of how I acquired this picture, but of what has happened since the moment I found it." She smiled affectionately at Annias. "I knew immediately that it belonged to the Ras El Khuden. Everyone has heard the stories of the search for a lost picture and I saw his mark in the back of the silver frame."

"Start at the very beginning, Magyar. The apostle will find the whole story most illuminating."

"Please do not think ill of my husband," she turned to Thaddaeus. "He is not a bad man, but these are most difficult times for all of us."

"You see," Annias interrupted her, "Hannan's men were the attackers in the square the day we arrived."

"But he meant no harm to you," she insisted. "I'm sure nothing would have occurred if Hannan had known you were there."

Annias nodded his head in agreement. Stealthily he cast a look at Thaddaeus which implied quite the opposite.

"We fear his brothers and must protect ourselves," she pleaded. "I'm sure the picture fell into Hannan's hands by accident."

"Of course," Annias said.

"Several weeks ago I happened to see him place this frame in a special trunk he keeps locked in the treasure room. Hannan seemed to be trying to conceal what he was doing and I was curious about what new prize he might have acquired. Two nights later he left the key out and I opened the chest.

"At first I couldn't understand what I had found. The frame was silver, but hardly a royal family's acquisition. Then I saw the face, and studied it a long time trying to understand what made it so different."

"The face bothered you?" Annias probed.

"Yes, but later I heard Hannan tell an aide that the picture could not be of much value and must not have been the object of Annias' search. Perhaps that would have been the end of the matter if I had not started to dream of that face."

"Dream?" Thaddaeus leaned forward.

"Yes, dream!" Annias answered for her.

"The face appeared night after night. I was not frightened

or disturbed, but I could not dismiss it. The majesty and the countenance of the face seemed to study me as I tried to understand it, and I knew I had to go back and look at the picture again."

"And last week you did?" Annias pushed.

"I studied it for a long time. Slowly I began to realize that some of the marks were blood stains. Still, the countenance of the face seemed to be one of a regal person in control of his destiny. I pondered why someone who appeared so stately should have such injuries. In an inexplicable way, I was gripped by the face. Perhaps my dreams affected what I thought I saw."

"Does anyone know you have brought the picture to me?" Annias held the frame upright.

"No one but my servant, and she is completely trustworthy. My husband's anger would be indescribable!"

"Your secret is eternally safe with us."

"Please do not think me crazy," Magyar pleaded, "but as I pondered the face, it was as if a life had become attached to that image!"

"Blessed be the Holy One!" Annias exclaimed, "Is this not the same as happened with Alicia?"

"Please explain what I have seen. The face is like a magnet that draws me." Magyar stopped and looked at the image. "I know you have the answer, great teacher. I have risked much in coming. Will you not honor my courage by helping me?"

"Of course we will!" Annias answered for him. "What you have seen is the face of the Great Healer. Etched in the cloth is the very moment that He conquered death!"

"Conquered death?" she gasped. "Can that be possible?"

"Yes, and He did all of these things for us. If you know how to trust Him, He will give you life."

"What are you telling me? Surely you must be talking in riddles or parables."

"No, my dear," the elderly man said kindly. "The whole truth is even more amazing than your most unusual experience. Years from now, people will marvel when you explain what happened when you looked into His face."

"Whatever it is that you teach, I am ready to accept it," she replied eagerly.

"The apostle is the one to explain these things to you. I will leave you two together in order that he may tell you everything. Listen carefully, my child! It is the most important message you will ever hear."

Overwhelmed by her story, Thaddaeus was really not ready to tell her his own. However, when Annias left the room, he had no choice. The old man watched from the doorway for a moment and then, smiling broadly, closed the door to insure their privacy.

The shadows were falling when Magyar again opened the door and called for her servant. Annias caught sight of them as they left through the front gate in the outer courtyard, and hurried to find the apostle.

"What happened?" he asked anxiously.

"I told her of the Master, of the crucifixion, the resurrection, the ascension," Thaddaeus said very thoughtfully. "I explained how He still lives with us through our faith."

"And what happened?"

"We prayed together that He would truly live in her life."

"Splendid! This is our very first breakthrough in the royal family!"

"I trust so," the apostle again said slowly, "but it will be His doing and not ours. We must wait for the morrow and see what comes back from this bread which has been cast on the waters."

Gesturing toward the door, Annias continued, "She is Abgar's favorite. Even his children do not have the access to his heart that she does!"

Thaddaeus only nodded as he stood up.

"She can be the means by which the truth flows to many families of great importance!" Annias gestured with great sweeps of his arms as he went on and on, chattering like an excited child.

Thaddaeus walked silently beside him. Seeming to listen, he strained to hear another voice, an inner intonation that would clarify the meaning of all that had transpired in the closing moments of the afternoon.

Two days later Magyar and her servant returned for another afternoon conversation. Both Annias and Thaddaeus greeted her in the small office. The brilliant colors in her gown were a striking contrast to everyone around her.

"I hide nothing from Emar," she smiled at her maid. "As Egon is to you, so Emar has been to my family for many years."

Both men acquiesced to the girl's presence.

"Like all of our people, I have said prayers to the goddess, Arinna, and to Kamrusepa. All of my life I have paid my vows at the great altar in the center of our city, as was appropriate for a person of my status, but never did I find peace of mind.

"In the last two days, there has been serenity in my heart and mind," Magyar smiled. "Never before have I known such tranquility. Within me is the confirmation that what you taught me about the Great Healer is true."

"I am grateful," Thaddaeus responded. "Such certainty can only be His work. You must always remember that all gifts come from Him."

"Perhaps Hannan will be very angry when he discovers I have returned the picture to you. Yet, what I have found is so important that I am ready to risk his displeasure. I brought Emar to you in order that she too may receive the same gift."

"God is gracious," Annias assured her, "and He wishes to bless all of His children."

"If she believes and will be His obedient servant, His power extends as equally to slaves as to kings," the apostle promised. "We are all one in Him and none of us is any more important than anyone else."

"And is it true that your Lord makes the sick well?" the servant girl asked very timidly.

"Our God is the source of all health," Annias assured her. "Whether He uses the herbs of the fields or the skills of the physicians, it is His healing power working in us that is always the source of our recovery."

"You said that the Great Healer made many people well just by His touch?" Magyar probed.

"I myself talked with the dead that He made to live and the sick He brought to health!" Annias became emphatic. "I know that He can make anyone instantly whole!"

"Wonderful! Wonderful!" The servant girl clapped her hands. "My brother who is crippled can now be made to walk!"

"Abgar will live!" Magyar exclaimed.

"Wait!" Thaddaeus raised his hand to halt the conversation. "What is possible is not always what is done. Yeshua did not heal everyone in Israel."

"But you have called Him the Great Healer?" Emar puzzled.

"And so He is!" Thaddaeus smiled. "However, we cannot presume to know how He will choose to work. What He does is according to His plan, which is more lofty than any of us can fathom."

"Now wait," Annias turned directly toward Thaddaeus. "Yeshua promised to send us someone who would heal Abgar! You must not suggest anything less!"

"I remember only the promise that a disciple would be sent to minister."

"No! No!" Annias set his hands defiantly on his hips. "All that I have done has been with the conviction that the king would be healed. I do not understand the strange things you are telling us today!"

"Then listen well," and the apostle's eyes moved from one person to the other. "One of the greatest perversions of the faith is to try to twist the promises to fit one's wants and wishes. Nothing will lead you more quickly from the truth than trying to use the message of love to fit your own desires. Regardless of how lofty the ideals may be, woe to any of us who tries to use the Holy One for our own selfish purposes."

"I know what you taught me two days ago is true," Magyar's painted eyes looked puzzled, "because my life is different. But I know that if you pray for the king and he still dies, the reaction will be violent and disastrous for everyone."

"I am sure you are right," Thaddaeus stared out the window, "but those matters are in His hands. We have no choice but to proclaim the truth, simply because it is the truth."

"No! No!" Annias pounded on the table. "I have seen what happens when you apostles pray for people! I saw astonishing results being wrought even in the temple compound in Jerusalem. When you pray, the king will be raised up!"

Thaddaeus whirled around and then stopped. Catching his breath, he let the fire in his eyes cool. Cocking his head sideways, he said softly, "We cannot bend God to our intentions. We must accept His will, regardless of what that may be."

"The king must not die!" Annias almost shouted.

Thaddaeus only shook his head. "Living and dying is God's business—not ours! We are to love Him for who He is and not for what He can do for us."

"I think I understand," and the bondwoman timidly stepped forward. "Is this not like being a good servant? I serve my mistress because I love and care about her, not for any reward. Should she grace me with some recompense, that is unexpected gain. Nevertheless, I do not work for what I can receive."

"Ah," the apostle smiled broadly. "Emar, you are not far from the kingdom of God."

"So, I am to trust this Great Healer," the servant's halting words seemed to fit together as she struggled to express them, "and be satisfied with any gifts that He chooses to give."

"And you are to love Him simply because He is worthy of your love," Thaddaeus concluded. "Let that be enough."

Magyar gathered her rich robes around her. "This afternoon I am to meet with Abgar, and I had planned to tell him of the wonderful thing that has happened to me. Now, I am not sure what to say."

"Nor am I!" Annias snapped. "I have been very carefully preparing the way for your visit. The right suggestions have been planted in his mind, but Thaddaeus is contradicting everything!"

"My friends," the apostle smiled kindly, "if our zeal causes us to promise something that He has not ordained, then we are only obstructing His purposes."

"So we are to trust Him, even as I trust my mistress?" Emar added.

"Exactly!" the apostle clapped his hands in jubilation. "The light is within you!"

"And if I love Him, He will do what is best?" the servant beamed.

"Your humility has opened your mind," Thaddaeus said very kindly. "Yeshua told us that from the low stations of life would come the lofty acceptances of the truth. Emar, your obedience will be the path to fullness of knowledge."

Turning to Magyar, the apostle continued, "As you have prayed, what have you learned about the Heavenly Father?"

"Our gods have always been harsh and ruthless. Perhaps the Great Healer is ever a gentle God?"

"He can be," the apostle said, "but He can also be like the whirlwind and His judgments sting like fire. Yet even when He corrects us, He seeks only what is best."

"He is a God of love?" Magyar ventured.

"Splendid! Only God can reveal such things! Yes, you have come to the very essence of the truth."

Magyar leaned back to try to absorb what she was hearing. Annias sat in silent consternation. Emar alone appeared excited and comprehending.

"My friends," Thaddaeus' gestures were as one who preaches, "what He does may seem to deny our dreams and appear to contradict everything that we desire. Yet we must trust Him to do what is truly best. Only as we surrender our plans can we discover His design. It is here that truth and love meet, becoming one!" He turned to Magyar and Annias. "The world cannot understand how such can be, but we must remember it lest we stand in His way."

"I have much to learn," Magyar confessed. "Perhaps I should say nothing to the king."

"No," Thaddaeus corrected her. "No, tell him the truth, but do not go beyond the light that you have seen." The apostle turned back to the servant girl and looked deeply into her eyes. "Today you came to receive the same gift Magyar found. I tell you that the gift is already at work within you. Receive it. Talk to Him as your heart dictates and let what is already in you grow into fullness."

Turning to Magyar, Thaddaeus said, "When you speak to the king, the Spirit of Christ will be with you. We will eagerly await your report. Now, go to Abgar with God's blessing!"

The apostle prayed before the two women departed. Then Annias spoke, "Surely you are aware of what we risk. If the king dies, Hannan has the power to kill all of us."

"Annias, Hannan can do to us only what God allows him to do. You stand at the place where all your diplomacy can accomplish nothing. My friend, you are in a terribly wonderful time when you will have to learn to trust completely. Do not avoid this moment."

"I have always believed you had a special power," Annias wrung his hands as his words trailed off. "Perhaps I thought that you carried Yeshua's power in your hands," and a disillusioned tone crept into his voice.

Thaddaeus smiled kindly and squeezed Annias' hand. "We do not control destiny." Before leaving the room, he paused at the door to observe again the consternation and bewilderment written in the lines of the old man's face. "A plan is at work behind what you see, Annias. Do not be afraid to let God have His way." The apostle turned and walked softly down the hall. Annias picked up the frame, clutching the edges so tightly that his knuckles became white.

That night the group of believers moved into the large meeting hall as others arrived. Annias' small family circle had grown in recent weeks to over forty men and women.

As Omri and Egon sought to make each guest feel welcome, Addai moved from person to person in a glow of enthusiasm. Thaddaeus watched the conversation and felt a deep sense of satisfaction. Still, his thoughts kept returning to Magyar's visit with the king.

Since so many new people had come, Thaddaeus began by explaining how Yeshua was the fulfillment of all that the nation of Israel had hoped for through the centuries. Although many of his hearers were not Jewish, they could understand the Hebrews' quest for a Messiah.

"I do not know what lies before us," the apostle said, remembering the uncertain atmosphere from the afternoon's conversation, "but I know that these days are counted by God, and no moment will be lost in His purposes. Someday you will look back on these events and tell your children stories that they will tell their children. You are living in a very significant time."

Omri raised his hand. "I would like for us to pray that God would give you special guidance about what to do next. We should hold you before Him in order that He will be able to fill your mind with insight."

"Thank you, my good brother," Thaddaeus smiled. "Such dependence on Him is the only secure basis for our independence before men. Let us pray."

After the group had prayed for several minutes, someone began to sing softly one of the psalms. The members of Annias' household and family joined in and others new in the group harmonized with a wordless chant. Slowly, an extraordinary hymn took shape as if they were both improvising and also being directed from an unseen musical score. A magnificent crescendo would be followed by a diminished wordless canticle, only to lift again into an emotional burst of joy. The sound and the force of the music swept the group along with its spiritual power. Near the end, the harmony blended into a final magnificent chord.

Each person was still absorbed in the afterglow when Addai began to speak over the sounds of worship. He was delivering a message from God to the believers.

"My children," Addai concluded, "go forth with boldness and fear no one. Set My face before the king and My glory will shine forth."

After a moment of silence, Thaddaeus dismissed them, "The Lord has spoken to us. He has confirmed His intentions. Let us leave in peace."

As he stood, others did also and quietly began dispersing. Each had been touched in his own way and none wanted to break the spell with conversation.

Annias approached Thaddaeus timidly. "Tonight I was reminded of how harmony always follows when the Spirit controls. This afternoon my own spirit was confronted and I have been humbled. May I ask you what you heard in Addai's message?"

"Well, I felt we were encouraged to proclaim the truth with boldness."

"Please do not feel I am trying to only manipulate or insist on my desires," Annias spoke haltingly. "Yet I felt that message was a word especially given to me. I heard it as a confirmation that I should take the shroud with me when I see the king. Still, I would not trust my ears unless you verify my interpretation."

Thaddaeus studied his face and recognized a change in the clever diplomat. Whereas the apostle had not heard the same message, he recognized a heartfelt sincerity and a changed spirit in his friend. "If God has spoken to you, who am I to deny His voice? We must each act as we perceive direction is given to us."

Annias only nodded and his subdued appearance did not change. He turned and left the apostle to his own reflections. Thaddaeus waited for the room to become completely silent and then sat down by the hearth.

Staring into the fire, he remembered another night in Jerusalem, one which seemed both so recent and so far away. Once more her face came into focus. As he wondered if Alicia fared well, a prayer welled up in his mind. When the apostle opened his eyes once more, the fire had long since burned itself out.

CHAPTER TEN

The ornate carvings in the stone floor and the elaborate tapestries on the palace walls had become so familiar to Annias that he no longer really saw them. He had walked those corridors for more years than he could remember. Running around the huge support columns and down the forbidding halls of stone as a boy, he had played games of hide-and-seek. Even though the palace had never intimidated him, today each step beneath the lofty ceilings increased his apprehension. He carried an object close to his side, as if to conceal it from any watching eyes.

Rows of the king's guards stood with their hands ready on the shafts of their spears. When Annias passed the soldiers, they towered above him, their pointed hats making them appear a foot taller than they really were. They quickly snapped to attention as the Ras El Khuden passed by. When Annias reached the entry to the chambers of Abgar, a soldier opened the huge carved door before him.

"Your most unworthy servant greets his majesty," he saluted the king. Walking across the room, he knelt beside the magnificent giant bed and placed his package on the floor.

"Ah, my friend, I am so glad you have come," King Abgar said, as with great effort he propped himself up on one elbow. Instantly servants were at his side to adjust the huge pillows supporting his back.

"Your wish is my immediate command." Annias lowered his head in submission.

"Come closer and sit by me," the king beckoned feebly. "We have much to talk about today."

"Yes." Annias rose to his feet. "I have something special to share with you."

"You have always been more of a friend than an adviser to me." The discoloration which surrounded the king's deep-set eyes made his pupils black. Seeing his large frame in the bed reminded Annias of how muscular and strong he had once been. Now his head seemed to hang heavily and weakly against his shoulders. His gray hair looked more unkempt than aged.

"My sovereign, I would gladly give my life if it would restore your health."

"Annias, to have one such friend as you in a lifetime is enough. Yet I fear even your life cannot keep the inevitable from me."

"We continue to pray for you every day, my king."

"Surely your God is my only hope. The gods of Osrhoene have done nothing!"

"That is why I am here today. I think the time has come for me to share with you everything I learned in Israel. I have only told you bits and pieces of my discoveries."

"Magyar has already been here telling me the wonderful things that have happened to her because of the teacher you brought back with you. I can only hope this man is the one the Great Healer promised to send."

"Oh, he is!" Annias quickly assured the king. "This

apostle can help you greatly. However, I have discovered certain truths that I must tell you before he comes."

"Excellent!' The king turned and gestured for all the servants to leave him and the Ras El Khuden alone. "Tell me everything. I am desperate for the truth."

"When I began my journey to take your message to the Great Healer, I was searching for a physician of great power. Indeed, I even talked with people who had died and were returned to life."

"Is such a thing possible?" Abgar sighed. "No one has ever done anything like that here!"

"As amazing as those discoveries were, I found that even more astonishing truths were awaiting me. While I began by believing this Yeshua of Nazareth could give life, I came to realize that He is life!"

"Surely you speak in riddles," Abgar protested. "I cannot fathom what you are saying."

"Let me see if I can explain my meaning." Annias leaned forward groping to find the precise words. "Do you remember how I told you that we Jews have always awaited the coming of an Anointed One who would become the King of the universe?"

"Yes, you always said this Messiah would teach all other kings the meaning of justice and righteousness. In fact, I always knew you used His example to chastise me when my decisions did not meet your approval!" The king smiled slyly as one does when his opponent's strategy has been exposed.

"After many days," Annias ignored the kings' barb, "I began to realize that this Great Healer is our Messiah!" Annias began gesturing with great movements of his hands. "However, people misunderstood the nature of His kingdom. He was not in competition with earthly kings for political power. His was a kingdom of the heavens that could turn this world back into a paradise!"

"What a most extraordinary teaching!" Abgar's eyes widened. "Who has ever heard of a king who would rule from above this world?"

"But that is only a part of His plan!" Annias interrupted him. "The Messiah extends His rule from within our hearts. He can change the way we think and feel and behave. Through His power, the whole world can be transformed!"

"I have always been taught to believe in military power and might, Annias. Treachery and deceit have been my security. Have not my wits served me well?"

"And for those same reasons, even now your sons would kill each other for the kingdom and set the people against each other!" Annias waited for the full impact of his words to sink in. When the king's head sank against the pillows, he knew his point was well taken.

"My king, this Messiah's ways are much better than the ways this land has been governed."

"Annias, I would allow no one but you to say such a thing to me. Yet, I cannot deny the treachery within my own household. But what difference can all of this make now?"

"A great deal!" Annias was fervent. "When this Messiah rules in our hearts, He brings us new life."

"New life?" The king leaned forward again. "New life! This I seek!"

"My whole mission is to bring this life to you, and in the last few days have I come to understand how to explain it."

"Tell me how I can obtain new life!" The king suddenly gripped Annias' hand. "I will pay any price!"

"Perhaps, my king, and perhaps not," Annias said with great difficulty. "The Messiah asks the one thing we are all the most reluctant to give."

"What?" the king snapped. "There is no price I would not give in an instant!"

"Would you die to yourself? Would you truly make Him King of your life?"

"Surely you speak in riddles again! How can I die in order to live? Such suggestions are absurd!"

"No, my monarch. You have come to the heart of the truth. If the Messiah made you truly well, would you then give Him your life and thereafter live it according to His ways of love, truth, justice, and righteousness? Could you, a king, truly give your allegiance to another, making Him your Sovereign? Could you, who have always ruled others, let yourself be ruled?"

Abgar's wrinkled brow betrayed not so much a lack of comprehension as bewilderment. In silence he stared at his adviser.

"We must die to what we want," Annias broke the pause, "in order to be able to receive what He gives. He offers a treasure which money cannot buy, to those who give Him what no one can take from them."

"What you are saying is so completely different from anything I had expected," the king began to speak slowly. "I do not know what to say."

"What I am telling you is utter madness, or it is the greatest truth that either of us shall ever hear."

"But it is not so much a truth that you ask me to accept as it is to abdicate my throne. You ask me to reverse every impulse I have lived by since birth."

"I ask you to let Him become your life."

The king began to rub his forehead vigorously. As he massaged his temples, his eyes darted back and forth as if he were mentally probing every aspect of what he was hearing. "First Magyar comes and tells me she has found peace through this new teaching, and I know she would not lie. Now you stand before me and speak of receiving a new life if I give up the absolute authority I have as king. You ask a price beyond any I keep in my treasury."

"I ask nothing, O great one. I only report what I have seen and heard."

"But you are asking me to believe in a Messiah I have not seen!" The king was becoming more agitated. "You come before me and want me to become like a slave, without any evidence but your word. I am a man who reads battle plans and studies the reserves of my enemies. Yet you bring nothing but a report that contradicts everything I have ever known!"

"Not quite." Annias reached down for his package. "I have a most remarkable object that may help you understand." Pulling aside the cloth covering, Annias held up the silver frame and handed it to the king. "This is a picture of Yeshua."

"A painting?" the king was puzzled by the strange portrait.

"No, you are seeing the imprint of His face at the moment when He defeated death."

"Death!"

"Evil men tried to stamp out His life. They too were threatened by what He asked of them. After they killed Him, He was buried with this shroud covering His face and body. After three days in a grave, He returned to life and this imprint was burned into the shroud at that very moment."

"Alive again!" the king gasped. "I am overpowered by such a story!"

"Yes," Annias said quietly, "the Messiah is overwhelming. Once we have encountered Him and His teaching, nothing is ever the same again. Slowly, but surely, the world will be made different because of all that has happened through Him."

Abgar took the frame in both hands and stared at the picture. He searched the faint outline to make out every detail of the face. "Burned into the cloth?" he pondered.

"Wherever He went," Annias assured him, "Yeshua left the imprint of life."

"Life?" his thin fingers clutched the frame. "Life—"

"When I began this search for you, I was only seeking a gift of health. Now I know it is unworthy for any of us to seek His gifts alone. The Giver wishes to give Himself, and it is not possible to separate Him from any extension of Himself. Truly He is our life."

"So, what do I do?" the king pondered. "Where shall I turn?"

"You simply turn to Him. You open your mind to the possibility that what I say is true. Just look at this shroud and let God do what He will. In the morning, I will send the apostle to you that he may answer any questions you have."

Abgar sank back even further into his pillows and continued to look at the picture he held. Silently he nodded his agreement and Annias slipped away.

Abgar found that the picture fascinated and drew him just as Magyar had said. The idea that he was looking at both death and life was intriguing. Reflecting on how close he stood to the same moment, the unfathomable message in the face gripped his imagination.

"I am not afraid of pain," he said aloud in the empty room to reassure himself. "Never have I retreated from any battlefield."

He tried to fill in the empty places in the image as if they might answer his questions. He remembered how in his youth death had been only another challenge for him to defeat. But now he came against a debilitating emptiness, and the void which beckoned to him was more frightening than any degree of pain. He saw again his dream of the night before, in which that ultimate abyss opened up around his feet. When he had felt that he was engulfed by nothingness, the horror itself had shaken him awake.

"So, You have looked into the face of all my terrors and returned again?" the king asked of the portrait. "I want whatever hope You give," each word slowly slipped from his lips, "and I accept it on any terms that You offer." With that declaration, he closed his eyes and dropped into sleep.

The business of the day had long since ceased when the small group of friends gathered at Annias' home. Though women were generally excluded from such intimate gatherings, Emar was there as a representative of the princess. During the previous weeks, people from a wide range of backgrounds had been present in the apostle's teaching sessions. However, on this night only the close, inner circle had been invited.

"Ah, Addai has arrived," Egon alerted the group.

"Come in, my friend, " Omri waved to him. "Now we are all here."

Omri moved over to give him his seat and the group of twelve seemed complete. Emar sat by herself in the corner as the rest chatted informally, until Annias at last stood up.

"My friends, much has happened to us during the past few weeks. Have we not been drawn together with new bonds and a special spirit which we now share?"

The men nodded to one another and smiled in the direction of the apostle.

"We have heard Thaddaeus teach us doctrines which have been revolutionary! Each of us has been set on a new course and it has been a wonderful time."

"Annias, for many years I have listened to your teaching," Addai interrupted him, "and I thought that maybe the God of the Hebrews was superior to the gods of Osrhoene. However, only in these last days has Thaddaeus really made me understand what you were saying. I believe you are all about to make a Jew of me!"

169

The whole group laughed.

"However, tonight I have something much more solemn for us to think about," Annias continued. "We are coming to a crossroads in our journey which, once passed, will allow no retreat. I must make the alternatives very clear so that you will fully understand the significance of what we are doing."

"Come now," Addai puzzled, "everything's going very well!"

"Yes," Annias turned and looked out the window into the darkness, "everything has gone well, but we are approaching events which could well put each of us on trial."

"Only in the last two days have I fully faced the consequences of all of my actions," and Annias turned back to the group. "I realize now that none of us can dictate or forsee what God may choose to do. He, and He alone, knows whether the king will live or die. None can fathom what His purposes might be. Therefore, it is possible the king could die in the very near future."

His words fell with a heaviness that immediately stifled the lighthearted mood of the group. "What are you really suggesting?" one of the younger men asked. "Why are you saying these things?"

"Should the king die," Annias chose his words very carefully, "events could move very swiftly and violently. A whirlwind might sweep through this kingdom."

"There is more you have not told us?" Thaddaeus probed.

"Once more I must confess that I have somewhat misled you, my friend. On the day of our entry, we heard shouts for my death. I allowed you to think that they were only sounds of confusion, but I have always known that they were intentional. A number of the princes would like to see my removal."

"Should the king die," Omri added, "our household

would be an immediate target of attack. They would say Annias had some part in his death and we would all be swept away."

"The apostle would be hidden and taken from the city to safety," Annias continued, as if the arrangements had already been made. "There would be nowhere for the rest of us to hide. Everyone in this room could be in jeopardy."

"We felt you should think carefully on these matters." Omri took the floor. "Perhaps you will want to turn back or dissociate yourself from us before matters become serious."

"Some of you are closely involved with life in the palace," Annias reminded them. "Addai has always made the headdresses of the king. Others of you are well known as our friends. The sword would surely fall on your households."

"I am confused," Egon said. "The apostle has taught us that we must be wiling to leave everything behind to follow the Messiah. So, if we retreat, will we not be denying Him?"

"But," an older businessman interjected, "you are talking about loss of life. Yes, we have seen and experienced marvelous things since Thaddaeus has come, but never have I entertained the idea that I might die because of these teachings!"

"Yes! Yes!" several other voices agreed.

"For these very reasons," Annias was visibly pained, "I feel we must consider the alternatives tonight. Again today the doctors told me the king's condition is grave. Tomorrow the apostle will see the king for the first time."

"Thaddaeus," Omri turned to the silent apostle," what should we do?"

During the whole time Thaddaeus had been sitting slightly apart from the group where he could study the face of each person. He had looked deeply into their eyes to see if

171

they registered confidence or fear, anxiety or boldness, strength or reservation. Intuitively he knew that the future leadership of the church in Osrhoene was being tested and tried in this moment.

"No one can ever completely know what will happen when the hour of trial comes." He smiled compassionately. "Perhaps you think of yourself as a person of great courage, or maybe you fear that a coward will be found lurking within your robes. In an instant, the fainthearted can become heroes or the bold can turn timid. I remember well another night when twelve men were gathered. Although each one professed undying love for the Master, by morning they had turned into frightened children."

"I fear no man!" Egon shook his giant fist in the air.

"Nor I!" Addai pounded his chest. "From my youth I have been trained to stand against all pain."

"I would never question your courage," and Thaddaeus extended his hands in an encompassing gesture. "However, you cannot yet understand the terms of this battle. A conflict awaits us of which you know nothing yet."

A voice protested, "Did I not grow up with the princes? From a child I have observed them and know each one well."

"Surely," Thaddaeus answered, "but the princes and their soldiers are only a small part of the conflict I describe. Our battle is part of an unseen war in which the very legions of evil are locked in a final battle for this world. When the hour of testing comes, an attack will be unleashed against your hearts and minds of proportions that the princes could not envision. That is the battle for which we must all prepare and about which you must decide."

A small delicate hand was raised at the back. "You are going to attack the gods of Osrhoene?" Emar asked timidly.

"All of the gods of this world are under attack!"

"What have you done to us?" one of the men asked in

astonishment. "How can any man stand such a confrontation with the gods?"

"In your own strength it is not possible," Thaddaeus calculated each word carefully, "because you will fall. Only those who have placed their confidence in Him will endure; we overcome only through His grace. The issue tonight is where we will line up in this battle."

"Please help me to be on the right side!" Emar pleaded.

"Such boldness comes only from a humble heart," Thaddaeus assured the young servant, "for surely the strength of meekness exceeds the sword in this warfare."

Standing up, the apostle began walking among them like a father inspecting his children. He looked at each man intently. Some he patted on the shoulder, while to others he nodded his approval.

"You do not know how to pray about this battle before us," he finally told them. "So I must lift each of you up to the Father. Let me hold you before His light that He may truly make your eyes to see and your hearts to perceive."

Some covered their heads while others bent forward. Emar dropped her face into her hands and knelt down until her forehead touched the cold stone floor.

"Father, the hour has come," the apostle lifted his hands upward and turned his face heavenward. "Glorify Your Son. In Him have You given us life and we know that it is eternal life to know You and Yeshua the Messiah whom You have sent." Suddenly they felt a burning earnestness erupt into his prayer as his words lifted them into a realm of unseen reality, where earthly matters disappeared. They were keenly aware that the sands of time had almost run through the hourglass of eternity. After the prayer as they filed out, it was with a deep awareness that no one could escape. Personal decisions had to be made.

The next morning the apostle arose with the first light of dawn. As though the prayer of the previous evening had been a conversation interrupted only momentarily, Thaddaeus again began to pray fervently. Believing that a fast would better prepare him, he did not stir as the hour for breakfast arrived.

When he finally arose, he did not choose clothing from the various selections Annias had provided for him. Rather, he opened a small chest in which his old robes had been stored. He felt the need to surround himself with the symbols that most clearly reassured him of his calling. Instead of appearing to be Edessan, the apostle wanted himself clearly distinguished as a simple Israelite. He dressed and went down to the great hall to find Annias.

"The hour has come," Thaddaeus greeted his friend.

"So it has," Annias answered soberly. "Are we ready to go?"

"This is the day the Lord has made," the apostle smiled. "Let us go in confidence."

"I am ready." Annias signaled for the servants and the two men moved toward the front door.

By the time they reached the courtyard, Egon and Omri had joined them. Several other burly servants completed their entourage. Choosing a side door out of the courtyard, the group entered an obscure side street and began their trip to the palace.

Reaching the large front gates, Annias stepped forward and led them past the inspection stations. Guards quickly moved back as the group easily found their way down the great halls and to the final stone staircase that went up to the chambers of the king.

As they climbed, Annias began nervously giving instructions. "We will wait outside and only Thaddaeus will enter. I will instruct the guards to announce his entry."

The group turned the final corner into the corridor which

ended before the great doors. "We will be waiting outside for you," Annias tried to reassure the apostle. "Do not be worried, the king is anxious for your arrival. The matter will be in God's hands."

Stepping in front of the group, Annias advised the guard at the door of their plan. The tall soldier went inside where he was detained only for a few moments. Then the door swung open and with a sweeping gesture, he bade the apostle enter. The room was shadowy and only dimly lit. Thaddaeus bowed his head and breathed deeply as if he were inhaling a prayer.

When he stepped inside the chamber, he could faintly see several men standing around the room watching him with suspicion. One official looked like a priest, another appeared to be a general, and one man was holding the instruments of the physician. The rest appeared to be servants or soldiers.

"Please step this way," a voice commanded.

In the center of the room heavy curtains covered the bed. As Thaddaeus moved forward, the curtains on all sides were pulled back to reveal the king propped up against pillows.

"His majesty welcomes the friend of the Ras El Khuden," the aide to the king announced in stiff formal tones.

"I am honored by the privilege of this audience." Thaddaeus bowed as Annias had previously instructed him.

Feebly the king raised his arm and beckoned for the apostle to come closer. After a few steps Thaddaeus came directly into Abgar's line of vision for the first time. He could see that the king's eyes were hollow and sunken.

"You may speak," the aide commanded coldly.

An atmosphere of hostility was stifling as the cold stares of the attendants clearly placed Thaddaeus on trial. The air in the room was stale and musty, as if no fresh breeze had been let in for days. With the windows closed and only faint beams of light coming through the shutters, the smoke from the candles and torches made the room foreboding. Death seemed to lurk in the corners.

"I bring you greetings from my Lord, Yeshua the Messiah. Your people call Him Jesus," Thaddaeus began. He tried to fix his eyes on the king's face and moved closer in order to be able to study his responses.

The king only nodded his head. His eyes seemed unfocused and Thaddaeus had the feeling he was not even being seen. However, the bony fingers again beckoned the apostle closer.

"I understand that much has already been told you about the Master and our faith." Thaddaeus' eyes caught the framed shroud that had been placed so the king could study it. "I see that you have been considering these matters."

As he spoke, the king's countenance began to change. His eyes seemed to be clearing, but he looked puzzled and perplexed. It was then that he first seemed to truly see the apostle.

"Perhaps you would desire that I tell you something more about the One whom we call the Lord?"

The king's expression now became intense. Thaddaeus felt as if the king were looking through him at something directly behind him.

"Perhaps I should tell you how He taught us to cast all of our burdens on Him?" Thaddaeus suddenly asked, without any idea of why the question came to him.

"Yes!" Abgar answered with surprising force. "Yes, tell me about how I can do that!" He leaned forward from his pillows to try and support himself on his shaking arms. The servants rushed forward to adjust his pillows and to assist him.

"We must dare to trust Him," Thaddaeus continued, without any plan of where his conversation was going. "We must be willing to take a step of faith toward Him."

"Yes!" Abgar's eyes still seemed to see something that was not there.

The men in the room were bothered by what was happening. The physician leaned toward the priest and Thaddaeus caught his whisper, "Is he dying?"

"We must trust Him to do for us what we cannot do for ourselves." Thaddaeus felt as if each of his words was pulling the king toward himself; yet the king's unrelenting gaze was bewildering and disconcerting.

Abgar turned the covers back and pushed his shrunken legs over the side of the bed. "A step of faith?" he muttered. Clinging to the cover, he fought to keep his balance so that he would not topple to the floor.

Quickly his aides rushed to the bed and pushed Thaddaeus back. Each of the men tried to be the first to assist the king.

"No!" he thundered with a forcefulness they had not heard in months. "Stand back!" his voice dropped. "I know what I must do!"

With monumental effort, the king stood on his feet, unsteadily grasped the side of the bed, and took one faltering step after another toward the apostle. At the end of the bed, Abgar began to breathe very hard and deeply. His eyes were so widely open that they seemed to be dilated. Yet he took another step away from his support. The aides stared in bewilderment.

"In the name of the One whose name is above every name, I offer you wholeness!" Thaddaeus pronounced with an authority beyond any that he had previously known.

The king took a second step away from the bed and then slowly dropped to his knees with such intention that all knew he had not fallen. Looking up to the apostle, he proclaimed, "Let all know that this day Abgar has given his allegiance to your King. I ask Him to take my burden and carry me through the land of death."

"By the gods!' the general gasped. "He is doing obeisance!"

"What shall we do?" an aide gasped.

Only the apostle moved. Bending down he placed his hands on Abgar's head and began to pray aloud. The commotion in the room stopped as each person watched at the incredible scene—a king in bed clothes, surrounded by his confidants, kneeling before a stranger who was in command of the moment!

"So be it," Thaddaeus ended his prayer and opened his eyes. The silence was ominous. Slowly he removed his hands and looked down on the motionless monarch. After what seemed an eternity, the king moved.

"He has heard."

"He always hears us." Thaddaeus offered his hand. "He always accepts our petition!"

The servants surged around the king to help him stand. Although his legs were unsteady, some strength appeared to be returning as they helped him up.

"Put him in the bed!" the physician ordered.

"No!" Abgar swung his arm toward a chair. "I will sit, as a king should."

Although Abgar had to breath deeply, to be at his table was obviously satisfying to him. "Sit opposite me," he motioned to Thaddaeus. "I must understand—" his voice trailed off. "Last night I looked at that face until I fell asleep." He gestured toward the silver frame.

"As I dreamed, I began to see a face before me. As I watched the face, the whole person came into view. This man did not dress as we do and the robe was strange to me. While I watched, this man stood before me and beckoned me. Again and again He kept saying, 'He who humbles himself before Me will I exalt.' "

"You saw the face in the frame—the face of the shroud?"

Thaddaeus asked apprehensively.

"No, no, that was not the face I saw. I had never seen the man in my dreams before—never—until you walked through that door." He pointed his finger toward Thaddaeus, "It was *you!*"

"Me?"

"Yours was the face that I saw. I dreamed that you were standing at the foot of my bed, in a robe exactly like the one you are wearing now, and that your hands were extended.

"When you stood before me, I knew that my dream was a sign to confirm everything I was told. I thought my eyes deceived me. You were as a walking dream. We have much to talk about." Abgar smiled weakly. "I must learn all that you have to teach me."

"And I have much to tell," the apostle answered.

"Look at his face!" an aide choked.

The sickly grayness was fading from Abgar's cheeks, as the color of health returned to his face.

CHAPTER ELEVEN

A.D. 35

"NEVER BEFORE IN THE ENTIRE HISTORY of Osrhoene has anyone ever heard of a temple of a god being replaced by
another religion!" Addai stepped briskly up the stone steps
beside Thaddaeus and Emar. "People throughout all the
region will be confounded by our meetings here."

"I would have chosen another place for us to gather," the
shadows of the massive columns fell across Thaddaeus,
"but when the king insisted we use the temple, who was I
to refuse him?"

The trio laughed together, each one keenly aware of the
irony of this temple, built for the god of health, now being
used by the followers of the Way. Each knew well the
uproar that followed when the priests had been dismissed
and the pagan symbols stripped from the walls of the
building. Reaching the top steps, they strolled across the
landing into the stone sanctuary.

"The statue of Kamrusepa will have to be torn down
before we begin," Addai observed, looking up at the fifteen-
foot carving. "That will prove to be some task!"

"And each blow will bring us deeper hatred from the

priests." Emar peered around to see if they were even then being observed. "They could yet prove to be a dangerous lot!"

"As long as Abgar is king, there will be no trouble," Addai said confidently. "He will always feel too much gratitude to allow persecutions to arise."

"Still," Emar argued, "many people continue to believe in the old ways."

"But when the king was baptized," Addai countered, "he took a position that none would dare challenge."

"Years will pass before our task is fully completed," the apostle told them both. "We cannot win the whole battle in a year, but in the end the victory is certain."

"I've seen many, many people gather in this place," Addai said, "and there is more room around the columns at the back. We can certainly have great public gatherings here."

"The table for the love feast could be set up in the front," and Emar paced off the distance in the center. "Thaddaeus could stand on the pedestal and preach—after the statue is gone."

"The room seems so cold," Thaddaeus remarked. "I would have wished, perhaps, for a more personal, intimate setting." After a long pause he added, "We had a special closeness in the upper room!"

"The upper room?" Emar turned to him. "What is that?"

Thaddaeus sat down and leaned back against the base of the statue. "In many ways that is the place where it all really began. In that room, Yeshua finished His three years of teaching and told us that we would be sent out across the world."

"And the love feast began there," Addai told her.

"Yes," Thaddaeus smiled, "and we had many wonderful times of fellowship. Much of what is happening here right now is as if it were all happening again."

"I imagine that nothing could really replace what the upper room was for you?" Emar asked.

"I suppose not," Thaddaeus agreed. "Yet I am concerned that the people of Osrhoene not think of the Lord's Supper as simply a new ritual replacing the old sacrifices which were offered in this temple. They must personally experience its meaning or nothing has been gained."

"We will instruct them carefully," Addai nodded to Emar.

"So many wonderful things happened in those meeting in Jerusalem," Thaddaeus said longingly. "A love was kindled that—" he stopped abruptly as though his words had struck a far too sensitive nerve.

"Is something wrong?" Addai asked. The apostle only shook his head.

"Observe," Emar pointed to the side. "We could place a special chair for the king over here where the high priest's throne was."

"Other royalty could be seated in the same area," Addai pointed to where other chairs could be set. "Prince Hannan may yet attend! I know he will succeed his father on the throne.

"Thaddaeus, once we begin meeting here, I believe you should have a title by which the people address you. A proper title helps our people recognize the importance of a person."

"What did they call your leaders when you were in Jerusalem?" Emar asked.

"We had begun to speak of leaders as elders. The Greeks called them presbyterios or bishops, but I was not particularly impressed with such talk. When people have titles, they seem to forget that we are called first to be servants."

Overlooking his reservations, Addai said, "I like that name. Bishop sounds like a very good title for you."

Thaddaeus chuckled, turning the suggestion aside. "What men *are* is more important than what they are *called*.

Anyway, I am sure that my time here is limited, so we can leave titles for someone else to worry about."

"Limited?" Emar asked anxiously. "You will always be here as our bishop!'

"When I came, I didn't expect to stay as long as I have. I may not be here much longer."

"Oh no!" Addai protested. "Do not say such a thing. You must stay always."

"You have been good friends to me," Thaddaeus touched them both, "but it is for your well-being if I travel on. I seem to have always been alone—perhaps that is the way God will use my life. In the past I have made mistakes that cannot be remedied. The day may come when I must once more become a vagabond, moving off to another land as God's exile."

"I know of no mistakes!" Addai protested.

"How could anyone challenge you, your life, your ways?"

"My errors are behind me," Thaddaeus smiled at both of them, "and should not be spoken of. Yet on some distant day I would not have this new church marked by any question."

"No one would dare come to us with any criticism of you!" Emar stamped her foot.

"Everyone should have such wonderful comrades!" Thaddaeus placed his arms around the shoulders of both friends. "But let us put such talk to rest. Now that we have seen the temple, we will know what to do with it. Let us go back to Annias' house to complete the rest of our plans." They turned toward the stairs that led down to the street.

"Still," Emar protested, "please do not ever talk of leaving us. You are right when you say that it will take decades to complete the work you have begun here. Do not forget that!"

They paused a moment to look at the city. Set on a hill,

the temple offered a full view of the city, all the way to the citadel and the huge gate.

"It will take years to teach all these hardheaded people the truth!" Addai was adamant.

"Well, then, let us begin," Thaddaeus said, as they headed down the street.

When they entered the courtyard of Annias' house, they found Egon, Magyar, and Omri awaiting their return.

"What do you think?" Omri asked immediately.

"I think we can meet in the temple," Thaddaeus assured him. "However, we do need to make some changes."

"Anticipating your instruction, I have already made arrangements to have the statue of Kamrusepa removed."

"Well, well, Annias isn't the only member of your family who plans ahead," Thaddaeus said.

"It is important for people to see the difference in the Lord's way." Magyar abruptly stood up. "We must decorate the temple to depict the contrast with their old religions.

"We—ah—were discussing this problem as you arrived," Omri made a feeble gesture toward Thaddaeus. "I have been trying to help Magyar understand our—ah—your reservations about such decorations."

"We have always used pictures in our temples!" Magyar swept her robes back like a peacock turning its plumage. "I don't understand this talk."

"In Armenia we had wonderful mosaics," Egon's voice rumbled, "and we were very skillful in decorating buildings with these designs."

"But they do not understand that we must not make any graven images," Omri protested to Thaddaeus.

"Friends, friends, please let us consider these matters carefully," and Thaddaeus gestured for all to sit down. "Omri is concerned because the Law of Moses forbids making any representation of God. Yet you wish for our meeting place to contain the pictures your people expect. I think we can find a compromise."

"People must have symbols to help them understand what they believe and worship," Magyar continued her protest. "We all need something visual to which we can cling."

"Are there not pictures in your temple in Jerusalem?" Egon asked.

"Of course, but we do not try to depict God." Omri attempted to sound authoritative, fearing he was losing the argument.

"Well," the old condescension returned to Magyar's voice, "I know how we can solve this problem. Let us place the picture of the shroud in a place where all can behold."

"No! No!" The apostle's hands flew up in the air. "That is not right. The shroud is not to be displayed!"

"How can you suggest such a thing?" Magyar's air was of one not accustomed to being denied nor contradicted. "The cloth is very important to me. And remember, the king believes it has great power."

"With all due respect to our king," Thaddaeus became even more adamant, "that is exactly what I feared could happen. Our faith is never to be placed in objects," his fist pounded against his palm, "but in the reality of the Spirit. The shroud would easily be misunderstood and soon a cult would grow up around it alone. If that should happen, I would not have brought the truth to Edessa. The old gods would simply return, wearing a mask."

"Then what is to be done with the shroud?" Emar asked quietly.

"For the time being, I alone will keep it." Thaddaeus' tone left no room for objection. "It was entrusted to me by the apostles and I will safeguard it until direction for its rightful disposition is given to me."

"Then what can we do?" Magyar was clearly irritated.

"It seems to me," Thaddaeus tried to be conciliatory, "that another symbol might be just as useful. Why not paint grapes or wheat?"

"Or," Egon suddenly seemed inspired, "we could make a mosaic of the cup and the loaf!"

This led to a discussion of what such images might mean to the people. Thaddaeus sat back and listened; he felt the solution should be theirs. His thoughts also went to the shroud; he needed to think carefully about this strange responsibility which had presented him with enigma after enigma.

After the group had decided to decorate with symbols of the Holy Supper, Thaddaeus returned to his office—a ground-floor room that Annias turned into a study and reception area for the apostle's use. In the past year, the office had become the center of the growing community of faith in Osrhoene.

The mansion gave dignity to his mission and yet his study mirrored the simplicity he hoped his character had come to reflect. At times the room seemed to wall out the world and its demands. Thaddaeus found that such solitude was important for his own spiritual perceptiveness; the plain white walls, and the austere furnishings provided a serene setting for his own meditations.

No longer was Thaddaeus an unknown who could make clandestine trips through the marketplace or walk unnoticed around the palace. His reputation as a healer and teacher had made him renown throughout the region. Now he had an assistant to sort out the many requests that a demanding public made of him night and day.

Addai had become his premier disciple and spokesman. Remembering the organization which evolved in Jerusalem, Thaddaeus gave him the title and duties of deacon. This allowed Addai to handle many time-consuming matters in the apostle's name. Addai took the position, not as an opportunity for self-aggrandizement, but as a mission from God. Thaddaeus was very pleased by Addai's growing sense of vocation.

As he sat at his desk, Thaddaeus thought again of the discussion he had just been a part of and was reminded of his need to spend time thinking about the shroud, its meaning and its future.

"Each time," he said aloud, "I have denied the validity of the shroud, a strange event has followed. But nothing has ever happened to me. Surely there is no power or enchantment there!" Then he thought of Magyar. And even the king had been in some way touched by the cloth. If he disposed of it, would he be denying future generations something of value? On the other hand, the shroud could become an obstacle. Finally he just shook his head.

"Excuse me for disturbing you!" Addai called from the door.

"Yes," Thaddaeus answered, without turning to look.

"A woman with a baby is here to see you."

"Can you take care of her needs?"

"She says that she must talk with you personally about the child."

"I am attending to another problem," Thaddaeus answered. "If she is a widow, see to her needs from our treasury for the poor."

"I will try, but she insists on speaking only to you."

Thaddaeus went back to his consideration of the shroud. "Perhaps my Jewish heritage makes me closed to the truth," he pondered, "or possibly my own reservations will not allow me to open my mind to see what is here."

"Please excuse me for disturbing you again," Addai interrupted his meditation, "but the woman will not be turned away. She says that only you can deal with the child's problem."

"Is the child sick?" the apostle sighed without turning around.

"No, it is a question of Jewish law that she insists only you can solve."

"Jewish law?" Thaddaeus felt irritation creeping in. "Problems of Jewish law here in Edessa?"

"I cannot help her and she says she will not leave until she speaks with you."

Thaddaeus tapped on the table in annoyance for a moment before commenting, "All right, but such interruptions only make my days difficult."

"I will show her in," Addai bowed.

"Please come this way," and Thaddaeus heard Addai opening the curtain behind him.

As he turned and saw the woman and baby, it was as if lightning had struck. His eyes widened in disbelief. "Oh my," escaped from his lips.

"I need your wisdom," she said very quietly.

"Alicia!" he could barely whisper. "Alicia?"

Silently, she nodded.

The apostle bolted from his chair and reached out for her. He wrapped his arms around both the woman and the child, embracing them in disbelief. The sleeping baby stirred and demanded space.

"I cannot believe it! I cannot believe it is you!"

Silently Alicia's dark eyes pled for her. Her face seemed hopeful, yet apprehensive.

"How—how did did you get here?"

"I came with a caravan from Jerusalem that has traveled for many weeks. A trusted servant journeyed with me for our protection."

"Our?" He thought for a moment. "Oh, yes, your baby."

"Yes, this is my son."

As she held the little bundle up, the apostle turned back the blanket, uncovering the face. He ran his finger across the tiny cheek and down onto the little hand. Instinctively the little fingers closed and held him. He could only shake his head and smile at the beautiful child. Finally he bent down to kiss the wonderful little babe.

"What a beautiful boy," he finally was able to say in amazement. "Yes, he does have a very strong resemblance to our family."

"His name is Joseph. He is six months old."

"Joseph! Named after my father!"

"I have come because of the child," her eyes looked down. "I must talk to you about him and his future," she proceeded very slowly. "In these last months he has become my joy and purpose in living."

"Yes, of course! But sit down here first where I can look at you." As she sat down, Thaddaeus suddenly froze as his memory began to operate again. "Is it safe? I mean, can we be together like this without danger?"

"Yes," she smiled sadly, "there is no danger now. We can talk without fear."

"How can that be? Here, sit in the light by me, where I can see you clearly."

"Perhaps your feelings have changed since I saw you last," she did not move, "and I will understand any decisions you have made."

"Alicia—" Thaddaeus stopped her, then realized he did not know what he should say or had the right to say. "Alicia—why have you come here?"

"Simeon is dead."

"Dead? Dead?"

"His own treachery was his undoing," Alicia said bitterly. "He betrayed a friend once too often, and that betrayal became his final error. I escaped with only a little money."

"What happened?"

"A great persecution swept through the church in Jerusalem and many of our friends were slaughtered. Telling you of their deaths is as painful as anything I call tell you about Simeon."

"Spare nothing!" Thaddaeus pleaded. "Tell me all!"

"For many months we knew that Herod was plotting to strike against us—even before you left."

"Yes, I knew of the dangers."

"Perhaps you will remember that James had a strange vision of a sword hanging over all of us?"

Thaddaeus nodded.

"One morning the soldiers descended on the city in a torrent of fury. Everyone they could find who was even remotely related to the fellowship was seized. Fortunately, many of our people were able to leave the city and they have fled to the four corners of the world."

"And James—what happened to him?"

"He was fearless. He was like a man who had come to his appointed hour and was ready to fulfill his destiny without fear or apprehension. The Jerusalem church will forever be marked by his courage."

"What did they do to him?"

"Herod's soldiers cut off his head and threw his body over the wall of the city."

"Oh, no! No!" Thaddaeus winced. "The world was not worthy of such a man!"

"His head was buried in a special place, where the church now gathers. Thus, all generations will know and remember."

"But why should Simeon suffer such an attack?"

"Your brother was a very consistent man," Alicia's voice was flat and distant. "He did not change. The night you and I were discovered, Simeon had with him two business associates who were members of the Sanhedrin and who had powerful influence in Herod's court. Several months later, Simeon badly tricked one of these men and caused him to lose a great deal of money."

"Oh-h-h," Thaddaeus sighed heavily.

"The man went to Herod and told him that Simeon was the brother of one of the leaders of the new movement and that Simeon himself was secretly one of us. Of course, the authorities quickly learned of my involvement and your identity."

"So Simeon was caught in the very trap he set for me!"

"When the soldiers descended on the city, they attacked our house. The baby and I were visiting friends and they hid us for the rest of the day. When I returned that night, I found Simeon's body in the courtyard."

"O Alicia, I would never have wished that on him! Yes, I hated him when I left Jerusalem; but for all of that, I wanted to make amends. If it had been possible, I would have made my peace with him."

"He died a terrible death. Even with all of the hard things that he had done to me and to many others, I would never have wished such an end. Even though he had given me ample reason to hate him, God would not allow me to harbor such feelings."

"He abused you?" Thaddaeus immediately wished he hadn't asked.

"You do not want to know. He decided that I needed a child to make better use of my time. Night after night, with great cruelty, he made sure that would happen. And he never ceased to revile me."

"Such things are best never spoken of again." Thaddaeus bit at his lip.

"I want you to know that I tried with everything I had to do the right thing. I prayed fervently that I would be a good wife, regardless of what he did. As painful as it was, I even asked the Master to put a true love into my heart each time Simeon humiliated and maligned me."

"How—how did you endure?" he fumbled for a response, not really wanting to know.

"When Simeon was gone, I spent hours in prayer. When I had opportunity, I received instruction from Simon. He helped me see that God had given me such a furnace of pain in which I could be recast. Many times he instructed me concerning the priceless value of a gentle spirit that he said was a precious jewel for the Master. I tried to believe that each hour of pain and loneliness was my opportunity to be transformed into the person I had never been."

Thaddaeus looked away, shaking his head in amazement.

"I prayed that I would give Simeon an example that would reveal the truth to him. I tried with my whole heart to redeem my error; I sacrificed myself for his transformation."

"Did his mind ever change—about anything?"

"No, but I tried to love him just as he was. Finally I could only pray that God would change me."

"God has dealt with both of us," Thaddaeus reached for her hand, "in the same crucible of suffering."

Once more his fingers touched hers and their hands clasped. Slowly Thaddaeus realized that while he thought he had known his own mind, he didn't—nor did he know hers.

"Have you changed?" Alicia asked apprehensively. "Has all the pain altered your feelings?"

"Yes, something important has happened to me. I put to death the coveteousness I harbored for my brother's wife." As he spoke, Thaddaeus felt a warmth he had not known for many months. "Now I know that the love I had for a little girl from Caesarea has been truly purified by the flames. Should it be possible, I now know that I could love my brother's widow with honor."

"I was afraid you would change." Alicia squeezed his hand.

"Oh, I have. Truth and love have come together in me in a way I would never have expected."

Thaddaeus leaned forward and pulled her to him. He looked into her eyes, searching for the very depths of her soul. In turn, her eyes darted back and forth across his face as though searching to make sure the moment was truly real. Thaddaeus leaned forward tenderly and then lost himself in their embrace.

Only the stirring of the awakening child pushed them apart. Alicia reached up to touch the scar on the side of Thaddaeus' face as he, in turn, felt the softness of her cheek. The moment was broken as the baby stretched and began to fuss, and Thaddaeus reached down for him.

"I often wonder what kind of man he will become," Alicia brushed his hair. "Will he have the hard nature of the father or the sensitiveness of the uncle?"

"Maybe there wasn't so much difference. Were not each of us only one side of the other? Maybe our competition was so violent because we each saw the other mirrored in ourselves. What I hated in Simeon I tried to ignore in myself. I loathed the malice that lurked in my own heart, and I think Simeon feared that I had found a spiritual potential that he could never again recover. We were both capable of the same things. The difference was only in our opportunities." Thaddaeus' voice became unsure. "You did love us both."

"What was love and what was convenience?" Alicia shifted uncomfortably. "It is not always possible to distinguish between love and want. In the very beginning of the marriage, I loved what I saw of you in Simeon, and yet I coveted all that he offered. After you fled, I tried to love Simeon and to put you out of my heart. I knew I had to do what was right. I prayed that God would forgive us if I tried hard enough."

"We badly tarnished the word *love*."

"Is it not sometimes difficult to understand what is love and what is only passion?" Alicia pleaded. She stopped abruptly and her tone changed. "No, we knew the law."

"In the end, truth always appears like the sun coming up after a dark night," Thaddaeus answered thoughtfully, "and we cannot hinder its light."

"So now, in the light of this day, what are we to do?" Alicia asked apprehensively. "I have not come to impose myself upon your life. Your mission must never again be harmed because of me. Yet I must also believe that my child has some special place in God's plans. I am here on Joseph's behalf. Even the law demands I come."

"At first I thought of nothing but you." Thaddaeus stood up and looked out a small window from which he could see the distant mountains behind the city. "Then I had to face my lust, my coveteousness, my own selfishness. Finally I knew that I had to turn away from what was wrong. So I closed the door and tried to seal shut what was past." Turning back to her, he touched her lips, "And I felt as though part of my own soul was dying."

"How well I know that door." Alicia felt the tears welling up in her eyes. "For many months I stood there."

"That door was sealed," Thaddaeus paused, "but my love could not die. Now the little one will be *our* baby."

"Joseph!" Alicia clutched her baby close. "Each night of the journey across the desert I prayed for the impossible."

"And here we are." Thaddaeus almost laughed. "My brother's wife, according to Jewish law, is now my responsibility! In place of a scandal, you have become my rightful charge. You are God's gift to me, His most special gift!"

"Oh, how strange it has been!" She clung to him. "Long ago by the sea at Caesarea, I believed our lives had been cast together. During the worst times I felt that we were being forced to walk through a furnace which could only melt our souls into one. And then it all seemed to evaporate, like a dream."

Thaddaeus drew her to himself even more tightly and cradled her head in his hands. She rested against him and shut her eyes.

"Maybe we ought to return to Jerusalem together," the apostle pondered. "Perhaps my help is needed there now."

"Jerusalem has changed, Thaddaeus. The authorities know of the upper room and no one can go there. Most of the apostles are gone. Simon is taking the Gospel to other cities, and young John Mark is traveling with him as his servant. It almost seems that God has been driving us out into the world. We cannot go back to where we were."

"That is painful." Thaddaeus stroked her hair. "I know that we must go forward. Perhaps Edessa *is* the place where I am supposed to be for now."

"I once thought that Jerusalem was the center of the world," and Alicia held him more closely.

"In those first days, it truly was," Thaddaeus mused, "but in Edessa I have learned that the center is never really a place. It is a condition He creates. If we are with Him, then regardless of where we are, we will be truly centered."

"O Thaddaeus, how did we ever get here?" Alicia looked around the room. "How did we ever get to this far-off country?"

"I think our lives must be like little boats that float on a great tide moved by a design that we will never be able to chart." Thaddaeus took her hand and held it tenderly. "The tempest can only drive us toward the harbor."

"Have we found the harbor, Thaddaeus?"

"I don't think we ever truly know where the harbor lies. We just have to make sure our boats are headed in the right direction so that the tides can do their work."

Joseph's little hand suddenly fell across theirs and clutched at their extended fingers. Thaddaeus and Alicia looked at the three hands intertwined and felt a sense of wonder and amazement.

"Yes," Thaddaeus finally said, "we can trust where the tides will take us."

CHAPTER TWELVE

A.D. 48

THADDAEUS TURNED TO JOSEPH as they turned down one of the side streets of Edessa. "The time has come for us to walk together as men. Now that you have reached the age of accountability, you must learn to think and act as a man."

"I am ready to accept any responsibility you wish to give me." Joseph's adolescent voice betrayed his attempts to sound mature. Yet he stretched upward trying to stand as tall as possible.

"You have always been a good boy, and your mother and I are very proud of you." Thaddaeus and Joseph walked onto the broad street that led them toward the center of the citadel. "We know that you will become a fine man and a credit to your family."

"I hope so," Joseph smiled broadly. He always felt so important when he was with Thaddaeus.

"Today I want us to talk about the distant country from which we have come. You must know about our homeland."

"Mother has told me many things about Israel." Joseph tried to match Thaddaeus' long strides. "Look, are not the city walls like those of Jerusalem?"

Reaching the center of the square, they stopped to look at the construction going on before their eyes. Workmen were carrying huge stones and loads of mortar up the stairs that led to the top of the wall. Building was going on in all directions.

"How long do you think it will be before the gate is built?" Joseph asked.

"They may have it repaired in a few months," Thaddaeus pointed to the hole in the center, "but it will take much longer to complete the wall around the city."

"Why are they enclosing the city? It will just make it more difficult for us to climb the mountains."

"Times are changing, my son. A great uneasiness is spreading across the land. The people of Edessa realize they must be prepared to defend themselves in ways that were not necessary before. We must all be careful and astute."

"I will study these matters." Joseph put his hands behind his back and bent his head forward as he had seen Annias do when pondering a problem.

"Now," Thaddaeus continued, as they began climbing the large stone steps on the citadel wall, "you do not remember how you first came through these very gates as a baby. Nevertheless, you must never forget that you are from Israel and not one of the Osrhoenites. You must keep faith with your family background that goes back to our fathers Abraham, Isaac, and Jacob."

"You and my mother have always told me these things," Joseph leaned against the wall, "and I have kept the Jewish customs, but I have many questions. I would rather not be different from my friends."

"I understand," Thaddaeus put his hand around his shoulders, "but to succumb to their influence would be deadly. We have always been a separate people who did not let the nations absorb us. We must remain so. That is why even our food and our celebrations are different from theirs."

"Are not followers of the Way freed from the old Jewish practices?"

"We are still Jews. We must be separate in a way that is different from those practices of the past." Thaddaeus looked over the wall and out to the desert. "Unfortunately, many of the Israelites thought that they were to be set apart as a sign of privilege and position. Their obedience became a source of pride and was turned into a mark of superiority over all other peoples."

"That doesn't sound like what you teach."

"No, it is not. Yeshua taught us that our separateness is to maintain the purity of our calling to be a light set on a hill. We are to be different so that we will not be absorbed into the pagan practices around us."

"Oh, I see," Joseph quickly caught the point. "We are to be different in order that we do not let the people around us change our purpose nor make us want to be like them."

"Ah, Joseph!" Thaddeus squeezed his shoulder, "you have great promise!"

"Will we always live in Edessa?"

"I do not know, my son. However, in this world we are all pilgrims and exiles, always traveling on to a better place than any which exists around us. I suspect the day will come when you too will carry our message on to some other faraway place."

"Me?" Joseph asked in surprise. "I have no special abilities."

"All of us have a special place in the great plan that our Heavenly Father is working out. In fact, I have always believed that you have a very important destiny. A special work awaits you."

"I have never thought of myself in that way." Joseph was startled by such a suggestion.

"The time has come for you to begin to consider what God may have been quietly showing you all these years. You should pray about His purpose for you."

As Joseph looked out over the vast desert that stretched south and disappeared over the horizon, and the hot winds blew across his face, he felt unsure of himself and uncertain of what to say.

"Do not be afraid to look for God's purposes," Thaddaeus assured him. "Only be concerned that you answer when you hear His call."

"You first heard that call when Yeshua came through your city?"

"Yes, it all began on an afternoon in Caesarea."

"And did my father hear the call the same day?"

"I think so," Thaddaeus said hesitantly.

"And that is why they killed him in Jerusalem? He was following this call?"

"Perhaps this is not the time to speak of all of the details." Thaddaeus stopped and rubbed the side of his face. He pursed his lips and then walked on very slowly. "However, I must tell you the truth. Although your father was a man of great ability and promise, he did not answer the call that came to him."

"He did not?"

"No, my son, he was never one of the believers."

"But I always thought—"

"Your father wanted to make this world his home. He wanted only the portion that wealth bestows. His purpose was to accumulate power and riches. He was a man of this world."

"He did not die for his convictions then—" Joseph looked confused and disturbed.

"Oh, yes," Thaddaeus stared into the horizon line, "he died because of his convictions. Unfortunately, they were the wrong ones."

199

Once again they both became silent. Deep thoughtfulness had settled over their conversation.

"This I know," Joseph finally broke the silence, "I have had two fathers, and what the one might have lacked, the other supplied. You have shown me the way I know I should follow."

Thaddaeus hugged him and smiled.

"Can you tell me more about why my father did not follow Yeshua?"

"The time will come when I will tell you of many things from the past that will help you understand yourself better. For now, let it be sufficient to say that what Simeon truly wanted he never found, and that he lived by what the world alone could give."

"Bishop! Bishop!" rang out from the streets below them. "Where is the bishop?"

Thaddaeus and Joseph peered into the crowded market-place and saw Egon pushing his way past people. He was roaring at the top of his lungs, "Bishop! Have you seen the bishop?"

"Up here!" Joseph yelled back. "We are up here on the wall."

The large man stopped abruptly and shielded his eyes with his hand. Once he saw them, Egon came bounding toward the stairs. Although he was very heavy, he could move with amazing speed.

"Come," he gasped for air as he neared the top, "come quickly!"

"What has happened?" Thaddaeus reached to help him up the last step.

"The people must not hear yet." Egon tried to whisper but his panting for breath made it impossible for him to control his volume. "A terrible thing has happened!"

"What is it? Tell us what you are saying!"

"Prince Hannan is dead!" Egon gasped into the apostle's

ear. "He was killed in an attack out in the countryside. Marauders surprised him and his men; most have been killed."

"Oh, no!" Joseph cried.

"I must go to Magyar at once," Thaddaeus said. "I will be at her house." He leaped down the steps and began running through the square.

"How horrible!" Joseph lamented.

"No one can guess what far-reaching consequences Hannan's death will have." Egon continued to breathe heavily. "All of us will be affected by a new prince who will become king in the near future."

"Some of the princes do not like us, Egon!"

"Things could change very rapidly!"

"Everything has been peaceful. Will that world disappear?

The large man shook his head as he said, "I do not know."

The next five days blurred together as both mourning and a state of siege settled over the city. Rumor followed rumor, further confusing the people. No one was sure who had originated the attack on the prince. While some felt it had come from the Cappadocians, others whispered that one of the other princes was actually responsible. The gossip and the whisperings made a tense and unstable situation even more volatile.

Each day the temple was packed with believers who came to pray for themselves and for the country's well-being. Addai led the congregation in prayer and worship. Magyar went into seclusion and the apostle remained close, comforting both her and the king. The believers watched and prayed, knowing that they would be affected by the king's selection of a prince to be his heir.

By the end of the week Abgar made his choice known. Fearing that delay or indecision could set off new conflict, he acted quickly. Though his health remained good, Abgar was far too old to rule with more than the force of his personal authority. Acting more with haste than deliberation, he chose Manu to succeed him.

"What will this mean?" Thaddaeus asked Annias, as they sat down together in the large room where so many of their early meetings had been held.

Annias looked tired and very old. He moved much more slowly now and seemed to take longer to organize his thoughts. "Well, I feel that I have failed us all," he said slowly. "I tried to prevail upon the king, but he is old and sometimes confused."

"You fear Manu, don't you?"

"He is rash and impulsive, and has been at odds with his brothers. He will use his power to exalt himself."

"What about Hannan's death?"

Annias said bluntly, "We must never speak of that subject for fear the walls have ears. The consequences could be deadly."

"I have not often heard you sound fearful, my friend."

"I am aging and my time of influence is past. The king's decision reflects his younger advisers. Very seldom do I now hear anyone call me the Ras El Khuden. Yes, I am passing from the scene."

"But you have been the king's best friend! Surely he will not forget what you have done for him."

"The king and I are both old men being overtaken by the young."

"Nevertheless, your legacy will be the eternal truth you have brought to this land. Our faith is now well established and its place in Osrhoene cannot be denied by a new prince."

"True, but never forget how quickly the political atmosphere can change. Irresponsible and arrogant kings are the devil's prime tools."

"What is it that you see, my friend?"

"While Manu is not one of us, he has not been our enemy. Yet that is not particular cause for rejoicing. He does not hold our group in any particular esteem and would not be averse to treating us harshly."

"Remember that there are now a great many of us," Thaddaeus protested. "The people would not allow a general persecution." `

"People are fickle," the old adviser shrugged. "They fear most for their own survival. Remember that great alarm has swept through the land. Should the king and his army be their only hope, people would look the other way at their indiscretions."

"So, how would the Ras El Khuden advise the apostle?"

"Put your house in order," Annias said, as he struggled to his feet. "You trust God so completely that you do not always think realistically about the contingencies of life. I too know that He holds all things in His hands, but I recognize that He also has left many matters in our hands. Think well about what He has entrusted to your care."

"The Ras El Khuden still remains the wisest man in the land," Thaddaeus said, as he helped Annias pick up the cane he now used.

"A new day is at hand, Thaddaeus. We must be ready for it."

Thaddaeus nodded and watched his beloved friend hobble from the room. Then he turned and went back to his office in Annias' house.

When he entered the room, he was startled to find Joseph bent over a large trunk, rummaging through its contents. Clothing was strewn on the floor and Joseph was digging near the bottom of the chest.

"What are you doing? Thaddaeus asked indignantly.

"I have always wondered what you kept in here and so I looked."

"Coming of age does not grant one the right to snoop." Thaddaeus pulled him back. "Some things are best left alone."

"I've never seen robes like these," Joseph held up a brown heavy woven robe and the coarse tunic that went underneath it. "Where did they come from?"

"I wore these clothes when I came here! Please put them back!"

"How strange!" Joseph held the robe at arm's length in front of him. "Do all of the people of Israel dress like this?"

"Yes," Thaddaeus replied as he took the robe. "I dressed that way in Jerusalem."

"How strange!" Joseph turned back to the chest and reached further down inside. He picked up a square shape and removed the cloth that covered it. "What is this?"

Immediately Thaddaeus took the frame from Joseph's hands. Although it did not seem possible, over ten years had passed since he had looked at the shroud. All that time it had been stored away in this chest.

"This is the face of Yeshua," he said quietly, holding the frame before Joseph.

"The Messiah!" the boy gasped. "Did He really look like this?"

"It is not a painting," Thaddaeus rubbed the tarnished silver. "The face is His imprint made in His burial shroud, at the moment of His resurrection."

"Can such be?" Joseph's mouth fell open.

"I brought the shroud with me from Jerusalem, after the apostles entrusted me with the responsibility of keeping it. Yes, you are seeing the true face of the Lord."

"His face?" Joseph peered into the frame. "Why, this must be the same picture King Abgar saw when he became a Christian!"

"No, that is not exactly what happened."

"All my life I have heard about the king and a strange vision! Now I am seeing the picture."

"The king did not have a vision of this picture," Thaddaeus felt again the old uneasiness returning. "The shroud was only in the room at the time of his conversion."

"The face of Yeshua! This is a holy picture, father! Should we not put it in a place of worship?" His voice had taken on a note of awe.

"I don't know," Thaddaeus said wearily. "I have thought on the subject for many years and have not come to any conclusions. I don't know, Joseph."

"I want to show this to my friends." Joseph impulsively reached for the frame. "I want to let everyone see what an extraordinary thing I have found!"

"And that is exactly what I fear most." Thaddaeus held the frame back from Joseph. "A thoughtless use of the shroud could be very destructive. Such impulsiveness could precipitate the very problem I dread."

"But father!" Joseph again reached for the frame. "If people saw the face, they would know our message is true!"

"And that would not be faith! Faith comes because we trust something that we have not seen."

"I don't understand."

"That's exactly the problem! You *don't* understand," Thaddaeus said tersely. "We will speak of this another day. In the meantime you are not to touch this chest again. Do you understand?"

"I meant no harm," Joseph said meekly.

"What we mean and what we do can be very different things," and Thaddaeus put his arm around the boy. "I know you mean well, but these are serious matters."

Joseph shook his head thoughtfully and left the room. Thaddaeus sat silently staring at the shroud.

"What am I to do with you?" he asked aloud. "I never

wanted this responsibility and have never understood why it all fell to me. What should I do?"

For a long time he looked prayerfully at the face. Then placing the frame back in the chest, he walked to the small window and looked out toward the mountains. He saw the wall that was being extended about the city and pondered the days that might be ahead.

"Perhaps we are all in danger of being overtaken by the young," he said to himself, closing the lid to the trunk. This time he locked it.

Thaddaeus walked briskly from the office and down the long hall that led through the rest of the house. He paused at each doorway looking to see if Annias might be there. When he reached the courtyard, he spotted the old man dozing in the sun.

"Counselor!" he called from the doorway. "I need your advice again!"

Annias awoke with a start. He peered out sleepily from beneath his shaggy white brows to discover who disturbed his dreams.

"I must make a decision and I need your advice."

Annias nodded his head.

"If I am going to put my house in order, as you said I should, there is a very important matter that must be dealt with, and you would know best how to handle it."

Annias again silently nodded.

"The time has come for me to make a decision about the shroud."

"The shroud?" Annias started. "I have tried to talk with you about it in the past, but you were always so closed. You will remember that I always believed it was very important—did it not prove to be so? Thaddaeus, its use is far from over."

"You are the one who most of all kept us from destroying it so long ago. I still do not know what to think."

"I never told you this," Annias sat up in his chair, "but I was so afraid that the face might be lost or destroyed that I had a ceramic painting made on plaques that I hid away."

"Always the conniver! Well, now I must face once and for all what should be done."

"Exactly!" Annias nodded his head vigorously. "The time is at hand."

"Soon we will have a new monarch. You have convinced me that no one can truly know what Manu may do. No longer can we be sure that your own house is immune from attack."

"Exactly!" Annias was becoming more animated. "Now you are thinking with shrewdness."

"So, the time has come to place the shroud in a safe place."

"Well," Annias hesitated, "have you thought about entrusting it with Addai? Or, perhaps someday Joseph will have a part in all of this."

"Yes," Thaddaeus mused, "I have, but I am not satisfied that they would understand what the linen truly means. I am not sure that I understand it myself."

"You never liked people seeing it," Annias settled back in his chair. "Your mind was always closed."

"I simply believed that faith must come from the heart and not through the eyes."

"Not through the eyes?" Annias pulled him closer. "You who were an eyewitness to the resurrection—you who saw the ascension—*you* say that what comes through the eyes is not a part of God's plan?"

"But faith means trust. It can't be proven or—"

"Proof never was the point! How the risen Lord chooses to reveal Himself is the crux of the matter. Is what you saw when He appeared in the upper room so different than what others have seen in the shroud?" Letting him go, Annias leaned back in his chair, but his bony finger still shook in the apostle's face. "Who are we to tell Him what He can or can't do, to let the world know the truth?"

Thaddaeus only shook his head. "I am too much of a Jew ever to be comfortable with any representation of the Holy, Annias. Certainly the shroud has been part of a wonderful work. Yet I fear it is too easily misunderstood. So I have concluded that I need to find a special place where it will be safe and not easily disturbed."

Annias blinked and stroked his beard pondering the question. "A safe place? Not easily disturbed?"

"Only a few people should know its whereabouts," Thaddaeus added, "and even they must have a difficult time getting at it."

"A safe place—" slowly Annias leaned forward, "I think—I think I know. I know exactly the place!"

"Where?"

"Over the gate—the gateway! The new gateway of the city wall is almost completed. Only recently I was discussing with the workmen about some symbol to be placed over the entry that would be a sign of protection."

"So?" Thaddaeus stirred uncomfortably.

"There will be an opening over the gate that must be bricked up. It would be a perfect repository—a hiding place! No one could open the hole without authority."

"What an interesting idea!" Thaddaeus snapped his fingers. "And you have the power to handle the matter in secrecy?"

"Certainly. Moreover, I could place my little ceramic picture as a decoration to mark the spot where the shroud is hidden. It could become a sign of protection for travelers." Annias reached for his cane to pull himself up.

"The dry heat of this climate would preserve anything hidden away in such an airtight place." Thaddaeus helped him to his feet. "Ah, Annias, you are still the master of every situation."

"I will arrange for the brick and mortar to be ready for us." Annias' eyes darted back and forth. "It shall be prepared tonight; then at sunrise we can quietly seal everything in place."

"Marvelous! Tomorrow we will complete our task."

"It is done!" Annias said, standing to call a servant. "I would count it a special honor to know that I have helped insure that the blessed cloth will go on safely into the future."

It was still dark the next morning when the five friends gathered in the large room in Annias' mansion. Addai was sitting close to Annias in case he should need assistance. Joseph was standing next to his mother. The early morning air was still cold and biting.

"Only Annias and I know why we are here," Thaddaeus began, "but it is important that each of us understand what we are going to do and why we have chosen this course of action. Joseph, please bring me the frame that is standing in the corner."

When Joseph uncovered the silver frame he exclaimed, "The holy picture! We are going to show the people?"

Thaddaeus shook his head negatively.

"The shroud!" Addai exclaimed. "The divine icon! I have not seen the blessed treasure in years."

As the candle flickered, Alicia bowed toward the image. "I can never forget the part this picture has played in my life!"

"These last days have reminded me of how swiftly the times can change," Thaddaeus continued. "Old kings are replaced by new princes, one generation steps aside for the next, and the tides of time carry us on to other ports of call. In such moments, we must measure very carefully how we discharge our responsibilities."

"If we put the shroud in the temple, it would be our greatest treasure," Addai clasped his hands prayerfully.

"I would take very good care of it!" Joseph pleaded.

"I am sure both of you would do your best," the apostle assured them. "Still, we cannot know what the next few years will bring. The time has come to place the shroud in a place of safekeeping. Only the five of us will know its exact location. If the time comes that it should be produced again, then you will have had ample time to ponder such a decision."

"What are you suggesting, Father?"

"We are going to the city gate to place the frame within the wall. We will be the only ones present as we seal the opening closed."

"But no one can see the shroud again!" Addai protested.

"Not easily, at least," Thaddaeus answered, "and that is exactly the point. We will also protect how this evidence of our Lord will be used."

"But, I see no reason—" Addai argued.

"Since it has always been the apostle's responsibility," Annias interrupted him, "it must be his decision."

Joseph broke the awkward silence. "But what if the exact location is forgotten?"

"I have a special tile that will mark the spot," and Annias produced the ceramic painting. "Any need to see a face can be satisfied by this representation."

"You have done well!" Alicia reached out to touch the little clay piece. "People can still see the face and remember. Even if they don't realize it, they will be seeing His true portrait. Perhaps something of the power I found will continue to work for those who seek in faith."

"Is this not a wonderful symbol of protection for the very gateway to our city?" Annias held the tile up for all to see.

"This must be completely our secret," Thaddaeus warned them. "Before God, I swear each of you to secrecy."

"But in that case, the secret could die with us," Joseph protested. "Possibly I would want to tell my children, or their children, about the face. Can I swear secrecy when I cannot possibly perceive what it would mean?"

"How true!" Addai placed his arm on Joseph's shoulder. "I will gladly die with the secret, but the future is with Joseph. We should not bind him."

"Father, I promise I will not reveal this secret for many years and then only as I am guided by the Spirit. Is that not acceptable?"

The apostle looked pained and perplexed.

"Thaddaeus," Alicia looked tenderly at both her husband and son, "is this not the beginning of Joseph's responsibility and perhaps for his own future? If he has become a man, is it not time to trust him to act wisely and prudently?"

"Then," Thaddaeus conceded, "the secret must stay within the family!"

"It will be so," Joseph pledged solemnly.

"Now, let us arise and go to the gate."

Addai helped Annias to his feet as Alicia gathered a robe about her. Thaddaeus covered the frame and they began their journey to the wall.

When they reached the gate, the grayness of dawn was breaking over the city. Annias needed to say only a word to the waiting workman, and he quickly went away. Slowly they helped Annias up the steps and onto the walk that ran above the huge vaulted entranceway. A cold wind struck them full in the face.

The gate's bricks and stones had been cemented in place, except for one square opening. Bricks, mortar, and a small box had been left for them on the walkway. The little group gathered around the opening.

"Perhaps it would be most appropriate," Thaddaeus turned to his old friend, "if Annias placed the frame inside."

"Oh, thank you!" he beamed, taking the silver frame carefully into his hands. "I remember as if it were yesterday when I had this made." His hands caressed the length of the frame as he turned it over to observe for one last time his mark on the back. "Those were the most important days of my life."

He bent down and placed the frame in the small box and closed its lid. Addai helped him lift the box into the opening.

"I too want to leave something," Joseph said, as he took a small cross from around his neck. Set with red garnets, the silver cross was etched Ιησους "This will insure that the meaning of the shroud is never misunderstood." He laid the cross on top of the cloth.

"Joseph and I can close the opening," Addai volunteered and began handing bricks to the young man. Together they quickly bricked the hole until only a small piece remained to be closed.

"Before we seal the opening with Annias' tile," Thaddaeus said, "let us ask the Holy One of Israel to protect and guide the actions we have taken today."

Bowing their heads, Alicia gripped Joseph's hand as she reached for her husband's arm.

"O gracious Messiah," Annias began, "thank You that You let me see Your face both in Galilee and upon this cloth. Thank You for the magnificent adventure that You have made of my humble and insignificant life."

"And I thank You," Alicia breathed, "that You used this sign of Your humiliation to open my eyes that they might see what my arrogance would have otherwise ignored—"

Her words struck something deep within Thaddaeus. A long-lost chord sounded in his mind. The shroud had always been a source of disgrace to him. The dirtiness, strangeness, and bizarreness of the cloth had violated his sense of propriety. The whole matter had always breached his sense of decency, infringing as it did on Jewish tradition. He had feared that people would want to use the cloth as a cheap magician's prop.

In that moment he realized that its effect had been quite the reverse. Those who had come in their brokenness had received consolation. Doors within the soul and mind had been opened when people had tried to ponder its meaning and message. The lowly had been lifted up and the mighty brought down. And was that not what the Cross itself promised?

All of these years he who had stood so close to the truth had missed the obvious. People could not be made to believe or not believe because they saw a mysterious image on a piece of cloth. Yet some who sought the truth had found in the shroud a source of hope. A penetrating sense of peace settled in his mind. True, the shroud didn't prove anything, but neither had it ever professed to. Rather, it was a silent reminder of the presence of the Lord, when life seemed empty of divine direction.

And now he knew he had the answer to a dilemma that began so long ago in the upper room. For a moment he wanted to snatch the frame out of the wall. As the rest of the little band waited for his prayer, he finally said, "Even when we could not see, You were watching. Your grace has allowed us to see what You reveal only to the pure in heart. We give back into Your hands our sacred treasure that You may use it in the future as You have in the past. Amen."

Joseph took the tile from Annias and knelt down to fix it in place.

"Finish the task, son." Thaddaeus handed him the trowel. "The secret is now yours."

Once the tile was affixed, all silently turned and descended down the stairs.

"Are you at peace?" Alicia asked Thaddaeus.

"I am at peace."

213

The group walked on silently until they were at the bottom of the wall. Each was aware that Thaddaeus was in deep thought.

"Have you come to any conclusions, my old friend?" Annias fell into stride along side him.

"Only this," Thaddaeus turned to the group. "None of us can ever completely know or understand the plan that the Holy One, blessed be His name, is working out. We can live only by trusting Him and leaving the final design in His hands."

"Will I be able to know what His plan is for me?" Joseph asked.

"Perhaps we never fully know except as we look back. Our only certainty comes in seeing what was," Alicia answered her son.

"But rest assured, Joseph," Thaddaeus added, "there is a part for you."

The five turned and continued on down the street. The sun was rising over the mountains as they walked into the new day.

Epilogue

A.D. 108

I AM JOSEPH. Once I was young but now I am old. I have seen certainty shaken and absolute laws tested. Mystery remains and endlessly unfolds its richness and beauty. Only God sees from beginning to end.

Although the days have been difficult, we have survived, and the church has not been diminished by its struggles. Thaddaeus and Alicia lived out their days in Edessa, and were buried together beside Annias where the great church now stands. Are their graves not four furlongs distance from Abgar's grave?

After Manu was the king for many years, he died and was followed by his son, Manu VI. The arrogance and brashness of the father was multiplied in the son. Addai became the leader of the believers and was truly the first bishop after Thaddaeus the apostle.

As a symbol of his authority, Manu VI demanded that the elderly Addai make for him a golden headdress, as he had once done for Abgar. Addai refused, saying, "I will not give up the ministry of the Lord which was committed to me by His apostle and make a headdress of wickedness." Even while he was preaching, the king's soldiers burst in and broke both of his legs, insuring that he would die.

His death was a great blow to the believers, and when further persecution followed, some turned away. Yet the rivers of Living Water continued to flow through those days, even to this time. Ponder carefully what the Living God has done, in order that you may better understand what He will do.

How do I know these things are true? Am I not Joseph, the author of the Scrolls of Edessa?

Joseph bar Joseph
Son of Simeon
Son of Thaddaeus